ENDITHOR'S DAUGHTER

DAVID C. SMITH & RICHARD L. TIERNEY

D0125125

FANTASY
ACE BOOKS, NEW YORK

An Ace Book

Published by arrangement with the Estate of Robert E. Howard

ISBN: 0-441-71159-6

First Ace Printing: October 1982
Published simultaneously in Canada

Manufactured in the United States of America

Ace Books, 200 Madison Avenue, New York, New York 10016

"Know also, O prince, that in those selfsame days that Conan the Cimmerian did stalk the Hyborian kingdoms, one of the few swords worthy to cross his was that of Red Sonja, warrior-woman out of majestic Hyrkania. Forced to flee her homeland because she spurned the advances of a king and slew him instead, she rode west across the Turanian Steppes and into the shadowed mists of legendry."

—*The Nemedian Chronicles*

Do ye desire, O symbols clear
And frightful of a doom unguessed,
To demonstrate that even there,
In the deep grave, we have no rest.
                    —Baudelaire

PROLOGUE:
A Deceit

The girl whimpered. From deep within her the fear rose in hot lumps up her throat; but the fear expressed itself only in whimpers, moans and gasps. She did not have the strength to scream. Neither did she have the strength to free herself although fiercely, frantically she fought against the leather thongs that bound her wrists and ankles to iron rings set in the stone altar. She shook her head, to clear the hair and sweat from her eyes, to try to see where her master was now—still somewhere in the room but in the darkness beyond the perimeter of lit candles. She whimpered again, tried to form words to beg for her life, struggled to sit up. But sharp pains bit down her ribs and legs, and she fell back again to the cold stone, to relieve the pain before trying again to effect escape.

Her master returned, his slippers shuffling on the flags of the floor, his gaunt gray-bearded face rising out of the darkness like some materializing phantom. The glow of the candles lit him from below, casting long shadows upon his face, distorting his features into a hideous mask. The girl watched him, eyes fixed to his face, searching for any further sign that he might harm her.

3

"Oh, *gods*. . . !" she finally choked.

"Shhh. . . ." He came closer, came around the altar upon which she lay bound, then stood above her and looked down into her face, resting his hands on the granite altar.

She could hear the dull clink of the knife on stone, as he rested his hands.

"Please, Lera," he said to her in a somber, quiet voice full of pity and sadness. "Please, do not struggle. Do not beg. This is difficult enough for me."

"Master. . . . Endithor," she choked. "By the gods, please—*please*. . .!"

"Quiet, I said." Still his voice did not rise above a hush. "I don't want to do this, Lera. Sweet child, don't you understand? It's the only way—the only way to destroy *him.*"

"Oh, *gods!*" she choked again, turning her head away. Warm tears began to trickle down her cheeks.

"Lera. . . ." He moved, lifting his knife.

The girl tensed, lifting her arms and legs as far as she was able, trying to shriek. She could manage only one, abrupt gurgle—no scream to alert anyone beyond the stone walls, to bring help running down the corridors.

And would they help, any of the other servants, if they heard?

"Shhh. . . . shhh. . . ." Endithor, hating himself, tried to console the young woman, tried to stop her fears. He brushed her golden hair softly, gently, as though it were his own daughter's hair he stroked. "It will be brief, Lera. It will not last. I must make the incantation, and then it will be brief. Don't you understand? We must stop *him.* You have lived a spotless life. The gods will not condemn you. They will damn me, Lera, but you will rest safely in their care. Do not hate me for this, Lera. Please. Please. . . ."

She whimpered once more, not knowing what to do, unable to hate him because he spoke so kindly to her, fearing his knife because in a moment he was going to kill her. "Oh, Master Endithor, *don't!*" she begged.

"Shhh . . . shhh, now. . . ."

Endithor looked away, looked at the dark room, stared at the ring of black candles surrounding him, at the altar and the slave-girl. He listened. Above his own heartbeat and Lera's struggles and moans, he heard no outside sound. None suspected. None had betrayed him. He would succeed. That—monster—would at last be destroyed.

Lera's eyes rolled fearfully, staring at Endithor; she sensed that he would say no more to comfort her. The muscles beneath her breasts tightened and pulled; her damp nipples winked in the candlelight. The sweat coated her like a salty dew, as if she had been splashed by sea spray, and her sun-browned skin shimmered in the wavering light like liquid gold. Her nostrils flared; she struck her head weakly once or twice back upon the altar stone, as if trying to render herself unconscious before the pain descended. Her legs writhed; her thighs slapped upon the stone; her heels scraped upon the rough granite, bleeding. Twist and turn as she might, plead as she might, Endithor was unremitting.

The nobleman glanced at a marked candle set upon a table beyond the altar. "The Hour of the Crow," he muttered. "It is time."

Lera moaned. "No! Gods, no, Master! *Master!*"

Endithor ignored her. Grasping his knife in both hands, he raised the point towards the ceiling, lifted the glinting blade above his head.

"Arkatu, hear me! Belias, hear me! Andomian, hear me! Ordium, hear me! Ye beasts of the Pit, ye demons of the infernal host, ye things that suffer dooms to

5

descend upon humankind, heed my call! Answer me, rise now from your dens and answer this summons to the feast!"

He slowly lowered the dagger.

The yellow flames of the candles on the floor wavered, though the windows were closed and no breeze blew in the room.

"Arkatu! Belias! Andomian! Ordium! *Feletek o doro semitu!* Gather now from the Hells! Gather now for the blood of the virgin sacrifice! Gather now to answer me and feast, and hear my commandments unto you!"

"No!" Lera whimpered, threshing weakly. "Oh, gods, gods. . . ."

Endithor swallowed thickly. With both hands he lowered his blade till the point touched upon Lera's flesh, placing it between her shuddering breasts. "Answer me!" he yelled out, as the candle flames whipped more and more frenziedly. "Ye things from Beyond, come now to feast on the virgin blood!"

"No!" Lera shrieked.

Endithor clamped a sweaty hand over her mouth, held her still while, with the knife, he cut a thin, shallow line down from her breasts to her navel. Lera squirmed terribly; Endithor held her down. Blood oozed from the thin cut. Endithor, still holding his slave-girl quiet, raised the gleaming dagger.

"Answer me, ye things from Beyond! Answer to the blood! Come and feast upon the virgin flesh! Rouse yourselves now and come to my summons! Answer the call and heed my bidding to slay Lord Kus of Shadizar!"

Suddenly there were noises outside the room. The candles sputtered and blew.

Endithor screamed: "Answer my summons to destroy Lord Kus of—!"

Lera, losing her mind, twisted and writhed, freed her mouth and bit hard upon Endithor's hand. Endithor howled and tore loose his fingers.

Lera shrieked: "Gods, *save me-eee!*"

Endithor slapped her, hard. "Answer my call, Arkatu! Belias! Andomian—!"

More noises—footfalls, the clank of weapons and armor. The candles jumped. Lera screamed and screamed.

Endithor waved the dagger, grabbed it again in both hands and lifted it high, poised it above Lera's breasts, aimed it for her heart.

"Answer my call!"

"Gods, save me-eee!"

"Arkatu! Belias!"

More noise—then light and confusion as into the room exploded a thunder of shapes. Voices yelled and cursed. The candles, extinguished, gave off curling columns of blue smoke. Lera shrieked and shrieked, finally tore one ankle free in her desperation and stretched her leg down, tried to touch her foot to the floor.

Endithor howled and fell back, holding up the knife to protect himself. The room was already filled with the glare of torches and the echoing tromp of boots. Voices cried out:

"That's him! Seize him!"

"Free the girl!"

"Hold that man! Hold him!"

"Gods, he was working sorcery! Look at the girl, she's cut!"

"Free her! Free that woman!"

"Hold him! Hold that man! Drop the knife, Lord Endithor! Drop it!"

Endithor felt hands roughly hauling at him from

before and behind. His dagger was wrested from him; dimly he heard it clatter on the stone. He heard Lera whimpering, saw her being cut free and helped up from the altar. Then he grunted as boots kicked him in the crotch and in the back, as arms grabbed his elbows and twisted them around, pulled him erect. Someone spat in his face. His tunic ripped part way down the front from the force with which the bullies held his arms behind his back.

"Bring those torches here!" commanded one loud voice. "Is the girl all right?"

"Aye, Count Nalor. Just scratched."

"She's cut, but not deep. One moment more and—!"

"Hold him!" Count Nalor yelled. "Hold him well! Bring those torches here! Here!"

A ring of flames surrounded Endithor.

"Do you recognize him?" Nalor called out. "I want witnesses! Do you all know him?"

"Aye, my lord. 'Tis Count Endithor."

"It's Endithor."

"Endithor, all right."

Endithor looked up, shaking his head. His eyes burned into those of his enemy, but he did not speak. Muffled pain growled in his groin and stomach, in the small of his back.

Nalor faced him resolutely. "Well, well, well," he purred, raising hand to chin. "What a fool you have been, my friend."

Endithor said nothing, just stared, taking in the black brows, the empty eyes, the snarling white teeth, the black moustache and beard, the entire scowling, demonic visage of his deceiver.

"Treachery, no less." Nalor spoke quietly. "Trying to assassinate Lord Kus, eh? And by sorcery! You're in for a bad time of it, my friend. They'll hang you upside down and cut you to pieces, slowly. Slow-ly, my friend. You're in for quite a bad time of it."

Endithor let his head droop.

"Have you nothing to say in your own defense?" Nalor asked.

Endithor took in a shuddering breath. "Dog!" he whispered.

"I'm sorry?" Nalor came close, smiling gloatingly, grabbed Endithor's beard and yanked his head up. "What was that? What did you say?"

More clearly, Endithor said fearlessly: "Dog! Liar! *You* told me to do this! You planned every step of it, didn't you?"

"What?" Lord Nalor's face twisted in sudden rage.

"Yes, of course," said Endithor, smiling bitterly. "What better way to get rid of a political enemy, eh, Nalor? Set him up for some monstrous crime, and then arrest him. Eh?"

"I don't believe my ears!" Nalor exploded. "Am I hearing correctly?" He glared around at his guards. "Did you all hear that? I want witnesses!"

"We heard, Lord Nalor," grumbled a number of voices.

"You're accusing *me* of being a part of this plot, Endithor?" Nalor demanded. "Is that what you're saying? *Answer me!*"

Endithor's only reply was a bitter smile. Nalor cursed and slapped the old man roughly across the face.

Still Endithor smiled bitterly. "Dog!" he hissed.

From the corridor outside came a woman's sharp cry. "What is going on here? Let me through, you fools! Let me pass!"

Nalor turned on his heel to see a richly-dressed young woman push her way through the crowd of servants and city guardsmen. In a moment she was in the room, standing still and staring at her father and Nalor and the rough soldiers. Fury and amazement showed in her proud, beautiful face.

"What in the name of the gods is this?"

Endithor stared at her, tears forming in his eyes. "Areel," he said in a plaintive voice. "Stay away. Don't get involved."

"Ah—your daughter." Nalor eyed the young woman critically. "Do you pretend that she's *not* involved in this plot?"

"Leave her alone!" Endithor barked, showing now his fury.

"What *is* this?" Areel demanded, approaching her father and eyeing Nalor angrily.

Nalor told her: "We found your father in the act of performing a sorcerous ritual upon this slave-girl. He meant to use demons to assassinate a noble of the state."

Areel's face whitened with shock and disbelief. "You're out of your mind."

"I'm afraid not."

"Father! What does he mean?" Areel held her father's head, stared into his pain-glazed eyes. "What is all this?"

"Apparently," Nalor said, a touch of regret in his voice, "she was not at all involved in this scheme."

Areel whirled to face him. "Damn you!" she screamed. "Explain this outrage, and then get out of our home!"

Nalor ignored her. "Get going," he ordered the guards. "Take him along to the palace—straight to the prison. I'll do the necessary paperwork. Get him out of here!"

"Stop!" Areel cried. "You're not going any—!"

Nalor growled and turned on the woman, slapped her rudely across the face, knocking her back against the wall. "Silence!" he warned her, wagging a finger, "—or I *will* find a way to implicate you in this. Do not interfere!"

Endithor was dragged out by the soldiers.

"Take the slave-girl along," Nalor ordered his men. "We'll need her as a witness. Oh, and stop gawking and cover her up! Haven't you ever seen a naked wench before?"

Sobbing and shuddering, Lera was hastily wrapped in one of the city guards' cloaks, then escorted out of the room and down the hall.

Within moments it was silent in the room—the guards gone, the nervous servants hugging the walls of the outer corridor. Areel stood alone with the altar, the stains of blood, the dagger on the floor, the fallen candles.

It was a dream—a nightmare. It had to be.

This had not happened.

She would go out the door, come down the hall again, enter the room, discover that the noises she had thought she heard were nothing, only her imagination.

It was a nightmare. It had to be.

This had not happened. . . .

Chapter 1.

Lord Endithor's incarceration was brief. By the following morning Lord Count Nalor had sufficiently drawn up all due notes of arrest, statements of witnesses, and legal proposals to present to the high court of civil jurisprudence. When the docket was officially opened that morning, Lord Court Nalor was first to be granted his appearance. His statement was brief and succinct; the nine judges reviewed his papers in the most cursory fashion. It was deemed unnecessary to call Lord Count Endithor himself before the podium to make any statement in his own defense. When his daughter, Areel, arrived at the court with a note of appeal signed by some lowly bureaucrat's secretary, the nine judges allowed her her say—but Nalor deftly parried every statement she made, discounted every flaw and miscarriage of justice she perceived in so extraordinarily swift a trial. She was overruled. The judges took their vote; in a unanimous decision, all nine of them showed the black card: death for the accused. Areel swooned and had to be escorted home by her man-servants.

Notice was sent to the public executioner to prepare the public square for a state execution that very afternoon. Nalor himself, in an uncommon abridgement of the usual procedure, made his way to the royal prison annexed to the courthouse and visited Endithor to give him the word himself.

"Put your affairs of the soul in order, my friend," Nalor hissed, standing before the bars of Endithor's cell. "The decision was unanimous."

Endithor lifted his head, and from the gray shadows of the corner of his cell his white eyes burned like funereal lamps. "No doubt," he whispered ghostily, "the decision was unanimous, seeing that all those judges are indebted to you in one way or another. They are not fools; they follow your orders and are rewarded. But I, too, did what you said—and now I am to be tortured and slain."

"Still sticking to that story, eh?" Nalor chuckled, though there was none in this cell-block—not even a sleeping guard—to hear him protest Endithor's accusation.

"You know it is the truth. I go to the gods a guiltless man."

"Not entirely guiltless," Nalor reminded him. "You were in the act of performing a sorcerous ceremony, you know. The high gods do not look kindly upon amateurs attempting to so manipulate them."

A long silence. The only noises were the damp hush of Endithor's breath and a slight clanking of his chains. Then: "I will be revenged upon you, Nalor. Know that."

"I think not. You die this afternoon."

"My spirit will follow you and damn you. I will be revenged upon you."

Nalor smiled sceptically.

"You are foul, Nalor. But your evil shall have its own due reward, and the Hells shall have *you*."

"Now you speak like those crippled beggars in the streets, who whine for alms and threaten the gullible that good gains and evil fails."

"When you die, Nalor—when you breathe your last—remember me. I go to the torture, but my death will be sweet and painless compared to your own. I see an awful doom awaiting you, Nalor—I see the fires of the Hells reaching upward for your soul—"

"Save your breath, my friend. You will need it for your screams, later this afternoon."

With that, Nalor turned abruptly and strode back down the gloomy corridor.

Endithor sank back against the stone, chains rattling. He was flushed; he trembled. He had made his peace with the gods, but he did not want to die. Over and over he whispered to himself, like a litany: "Remember what I say, Nalor. The Hells will be your reward. When you die, remember me. When you die, you *will* remember me. . . ."

Nalor was not present at the court when, later that morning, Areel returned with a summons, this time signed by her local magistrate, demanding to see her father one last time before he was taken to be executed. But even with Nalor absent, the nine dark judges did as they knew the nobleman would have wished. They denied Areel her visit.

"You cannot do this!" cried Areel, outraged. "It is against the law you are supposed to uphold! Every prisoner is allowed one visit by his kin before his execution."

The judges huddled together and murmured for a moment; then the chief of them announced: "That is so, save for two instances. Firstly, your father is convicted of a treasonable crime, and a crime against the state or any of its officers disallows any of the usual

14

leniencies. Secondly, no visits are allowed during the final twenty-four hours preceding the execution; we are now within that period."

"This is monstrous!" Areel protested. "He was arrested only last night, and sentenced this morning. He will be dead before a day and a night have elapsed since his arrest. It is mockery!"

"Silence!" The foremost judge stood up, slapping his hands on his podium. "Silence, or you will be escorted from this hall! I advise you to get yourself home and pray to the gods for your father's spirit. He is a wicked man, a sorcerer, and will need your intervention if he is not to be damned to the eternal Hells. Now, get you gone! Our business is pressing, and we have already given too much time and attention to the offspring of a traitor."

Endithor's apartment, in the most exclusive section of Shadizar, overlooking the main offices and buildings of government, gave Areel a clear view of the main square where the execution was to take place. She sat alone in a high chamber, at an open window, watching as the sentence was carried out.

Public bills had been posted all morning; by noon the square was beginning to fill with the throngs of curious, and the merchants' stalls were doing better than they had done all year. Flagons of wine were lifted high, cheeses and cakes devoured, songs sung, lutes and flutes played. The pickpockets of the city, too, were managing more business in a few hours than most had garnered for the entire past twelvemonth. The skies began clouding around noon; within the hour a light drizzle began to sprinkle upon the city, but did not in the least affect the gathering crowds.

Areel shed no tears. She did not mourn, nor wail her

anguish. She was her father's daughter, raised to endure all things with quiet pride. Court life had taught her father to maintain an outward dignity and a strong reliance on one's own self; and Endithor had bequeathed this outlook to his daughter. Areel was stone; she was steel, and fire. Good and bad alike passed before her critical attention to gain only a mute acknolwedgement in her expression. Few things brought her to despair, fewer things still lifted her to heights of unrestrained emotion. That sort of existence was for those who had little to lose, little to gain; Areel had been raised in a world of wealth and power and intrigue, and she had everything to protect, herself first of all.

As the horns trumpeted outside, announcing the beginning of the execution, Areel set aside the books she had been examining: her father's diaries and records. They told her everything: Nalor's treachery—her father's fear of Kus, the mysterious nobleman who either controlled Nalor or was controlled by him—the long history of Nalor's gradual attainment of power in court, and his evil use of that power—all of it was in the records her father had kept. The last entry had been recorded yesterday, as dutifully as all the rest; in his spidery Zamoran script Endithor had noted his intended act of sorcery, his decision to sacrifice Lera for the good of the community, and his brief acknowledgement of the gods, along with a prayer for their understanding of his actions.

The trumpets blared again. Areel leaned upon the sill, looked down upon the distant crowds. A government official, dressed in scarlet and gold, rode through the throng on a white steed, then dismounted and climbed the steps of the tall stage erected in the middle of the square.

At that moment, someone knocked on Areel's door. She turned, angry. "I told you that I wished to be left alone!"

"Pardon, mistress." The voice was that of one of her man-servants. "It is important."

"More important than my father's death?" she snarled. But, acquiescing: "Enter!"

The man opened the door and bowed. He was middle-aged and wore the tunic of a head servant. "May I speak, mistress?" he asked.

Areel nodded.

"Mistress, I thought you should know that many of the servants of your household have left the premises."

"What do you mean?"

"They are gone. Only six remain—the steward, one stable-boy, two slaves, myself, and the girl."

"Lera?"

"She has remained."

"And the others?"

The man-servant shrugged. "They must have left this morning. Their personal things are gone from their quarters."

Areel sneered. "Didn't want to serve any longer in the house of a traitor, eh? What about the rest of you, Tirs? Are you going to run, as well?"

The man's head lifted with pride. "We are yours. The slaves must remain, and so long as you pay the remainder of us for our services, we will stay also."

"Very well—" Another trumpet blast sounded from outside. "Leave me now, Tirs."

"Very good, mistress." The man bowed and backed out, shut the door.

Areel returned to the window and watched the square. The official on the stage was making some last announcement about the execution of Lord Count

Endithor of Shadizar. Another series of trumpet blasts, and then the crowds cheered as a horse and cart made its way through the square from the direction of the royal prison. Endithor, bound with chains hand and foot, crouched huddled in the cart as missiles thrown by the mob sailed over him. The horse and cart paused at the steps of the platform; two guards unlatched the cart and dragged the prisoner out. Rocks, vegetables and clods of mud struck Endithor and his guards, as well. A troop of soldiers surrounded the stage and warded back the crowds, and Endithor was walked to the center of the platform and shown all around, to the citizens of Shadizar.

More rocks and vegetables flew. Mounted troops pushed the crowds farther back. Then, following the path of the horse and cart, an escort from the palace brought the state executioner into the square. After another announcement, he was led up the stairs—a huge man, naked save for a dark loincloth strapped beneath his large belly by means of a wide leather belt, his identity hidden by a black hood reaching half-way down his chest and back. In his large hands he carried a number of grim-looking tools of torture.

Several guards mounted the stage after him. They stripped Endithor naked, attached long chains to the manacles at his ankles, looped these chains to pulleys set in the gallows of the stage. Roughly they hauled the doomed man up, cranking the chains with a windlass. When finally Endithor was hanging upside down by his ankles, his wrists were freed; his arms were stretched apart and attached to large staples in the stage.

The crowd cheered. The city soldiers trooped down the stairs and took up positions with their fellows before the stage, holding back the mob. And then the royal executioner began to apply his trade.

18

He was master at it—master not only at creating agony in his victims, but also in gauging the response of the crowd. With a showman's instincts the anonymous executioner led them on, building up their interest, drawing blood or wrenching limbs with a subtle, slow build-up of savage artfulness. The screams he drew from Endithor rose in pitch and duration exactly to complement the rising, gleeful excitement of the packed mob.

First came a scourging—nothing drastic—concentrating on Lord Endithor's face and genitals. Then, small cuts were made upon his face, his hands and soles of his feet, followed by deeper cuts down his sides, front and back. This was followed up by hot pincers, applied here and there for maximum pain. More scourging ensued, this time with barbed leather, after which salts and burning spices were rubbed into the wounds. Then, returning to the white-hot pincers, the executioner commenced the joint-by-joint dismemberment of toes and fingers. And finally, serious work upon the face began—slow and careful gouging and cutting that disfigured and blinded without affecting the vocal regions. Countless screams of pain rose to the drizzling skies, together with the mob's wildly enthusiastic cheers.

Areel watched to the last—watched mutely, with fierce hatred boiling within her. She felt the hate growing silently, like another self, as sabers and saws ripped muscles from Endithor's legs and arms and back, as the scalp was ripped from his skull, as— finally—his belly was slashed, his limbs dismembered, his head cut free and mounted on a pole.

That such atrocities could be did not amaze her, for along with all members of her class and race she had witnessed such violent executions many times. It was no worse than what most criminals condemned to death went through.

But this time, it was her father! Though she witnessed it stoically enough, from outward appearances, this was the execution of her father—and he was innocent. Innocent!

While the court which had condemned him went free.

While Nalor, the man who owned and controlled that court, went unhampered along his way, concocting new crimes, doing as he pleased.

When the execution was over, Areel closed the shutters of her window and sat there throughout the long, gray afternoon, reliving the agonies in her mind as an incentive to her own already-forming plans of revenge. That her own life was in danger she did not doubt. How long would Nalor allow her, Endithor's daughter, to live, when she provided a constant threat to him?

But Nalor, she knew, would not act immediately. That would arouse suspicion. And so she would have time to form her own plan of retribution.

Yet her mind formed no certain course of action, created no real schedule—until, late that evening, she returned to her room and perused her father's diaries and journals.

For the first time, she opened many strange old books and scrolls she had not suspected he had owned. Then Areel was quietly stunned. For, whatever her father's motivation or goal, these books proved without a doubt that he had indeed practiced sorcery.

Areel began to read the books, and her plan formed. To fight Nalor on his own ground—with lawyers, with legal maneuvers and other such mundane devices— would only invite certain defeat.

But to battle him with sorcery—?

Aye, she would fight him with potions and spells, with influences and evils beyond his own pale, earthly imitation of evil! She would carry on her father's unfinished work. She would utterly destroy Nalor, body *and* spirit, by means of such things as only damned and desperate souls resort to.

Her eyes blazed with fierce excitement. "I shall!" she cried aloud. "I have no other true choice!"

There was little time; she must act swiftly; she must employ tools of whose efficacy there could be no doubt whatsoever.

"Sorcery!" she muttered.

Sorcery, to destroy the man who had destroyed her father.

She looked to her father's books, lit a few extra oil lamps against the encroaching darkness of her room, and applied herself again to the ancient grimoires.

At the same moment, not far away, Lord Count Nalor ate a late supper in a small private chamber of his apartment. A single lute-player provided accompaniment, strumming a sad tune about parted lovers. Half-way through the song, a slave jangled a bell and entered the room. Nalor looked up.

"Lord Kus, master."

Nalor nodded. The servant side-stepped, somewhat nervously, and Kus entered.

He was a tall, thin-faced man, strikingly pale, dressed in muted purples and golds. His dark, unblinking eyes suggested a touch of sinister humor. Without a word he took his place in a chair opposite Nalor's; the servant who had announced him followed in a moment with a silver tray containing only a stoppered flask and a golden goblet. When the servant bowed low and exited, Kus—under Nalor's watchful eye—unstoppered the flask and poured himself a cup of dark liquid that was too red and thick to be wine.

Nalor squirmed slightly and averted his face as Kus raised the goblet to his lips and sipped from it. Kus smiled, wiped his lips with a napkin.

"It distresses you to see me drink that?"

"It distresses me, yes."

Kus laughed, a throaty growl. "Why? In your own way, you're certainly as much a blood-sucker as I. Survive on a battlefield sometime, like I did, and live on human blood and flesh for your only sustenance while your body repairs itself. You'll learn to drink blood."

"That was a long time ago."

"I became very used to it." Kus raised the goblet once more. Nalor could not watch him; he set down his fork, reached for his own goblet, then moved his hand away. He turned to his musician and commanded him to play something cheerier. Then, facing Kus again, he commented:

"It was done today."

"Endithor?"

"Yes. We arrested him last night. The judges posed no problem whatever, and he was executed this afternoon. The crowd loved it."

"No doubt." Kus smiled, a dark gleam in his eye. "Then we are safe. No one else suspects."

"I'm not so sure," said Nalor. "I'm worried about his daughter."

"Oh? And what does she know?"

"Nothing, I'm sure. But she hates me. She fought me in court today, and I know that she returned later to try to see the old man. I'm certain she won't let the matter rest."

Kus shrugged. "It is not of pressing importance."

"No, no. But in time, I'd like to see her removed. Just to insure our own safety."

Kus smiled slowly. "Good, my friend. Good. Let her

sit for a while; and then, when the time comes—" He raised his goblet to his lips once more.

Nalor shuddered involuntarily, looked Kus in the eyes. They were malignant eyes. Quickly he looked away—and toyed with his food, and ignored his wine goblet. . . .

The Dragon Seed Tavern tonight was in robust good health, swarming with patrons who laughed and talked and spent money, reliving again and again all the fine details of Lord Count Endithor's execution. Stout Obis, the proprietor, stood behind his counter and watched his serving girls hurry with their orders and smiled and smiled. Gold and silver jangled everywhere.

"It was a good show!" commented one rogue, sitting with companions at a shadowed table. "The executioner took his time—put on a good display." He adjusted the headband which covered the loss of one eye, then sipped his beer.

"And a good thing, too, that he took his time," piped up a rat-faced thief next to him, "for it gave me the more time to take *my* pickings, by Bel!" He pulled out his purse, which was overflowing, and ordered more cups around.

Across from them sat a burly, hairy-bellied rogue whose head was nestled comfortably between the large breasts of the wench standing behind him. "I find it hard to believe," he commented, "that Endithor was as guilty of those crimes as the proclamation stated. Now, I'm a seasoned man, by Anu!—experienced in the ways of the world. I can sense the rotten smell of vice and intrigue as the forest animals sense hunters on their trail! Endithor was only a minor noble. My hunch is that he stumbled onto somebody's secret, and that the charges were trumped up to make an example of him.

He got too close to the bones in somebody's boudoir!"

The one-eyed man frowned and nodded. "Aye, 'tis very possible. The difference between those upper-crust dogs and us, simply put, is that they're not honest about their dishonesty."

"What has the world come to," wondered the rat-faced man aloud, "when there are more thieves in public office than there are on the city streets?"

The burly rogue guffawed at that and slapped the table; cups danced and beer spilled over their rims. He slurped down the last of his own, then reached up to squeeze the left breast of his wench. "Get us some more, Viona," he growled, handing her a pocketful of coppers.

As the girl passed through the crowded tavern, she could hear at every table similar conversations. Lord Endithor's execution was the news of the hour, and everyone had an opinion.

But at the opposite side of the bar, games were going on. Here the players were much more intent in racking up their points than in reliving the day's past excitement. A small knot of people, those who had fallen out of the competition, surrounded the final two players: a blond-haired man in Corinthian armor and a tall, red-haired woman wearing a sleeveless tunic of chain mail. The man—just one of the many outlanders who had found a home in Shadizar's port of lost souls—gave an eye to his opponent and stepped up to the line. The woman, smirking, stood back and borrowed a sip from a wine cup behind her, then watched quietly.

The blond Corinthian took his time, lifting his knife and holding it poised handle in the air, concentrating on the bull's eye painted on the wall several paces before him. The innumerable cracks and dents patterned on the rings he tried, in his concentration, to congeal into a path that would lead his knife straight to the center. He took in a breath, held it—then, with a sure jerk of his wrist, flip-threw the knife. It spun and struck, straight in the center of the bull's eye.

"Well done, Sendes!" laughed one of his companions, slapping him on the back. "Ten points! You've won!"

"Not yet," countered another. "If Sonja makes the bull's eye, she's got him by three points."

Sendes stepped back, retrieved his beer from his table and swallowed a long draft. He eyed the woman called Sonja, who still stood with arms crossed over her breasts, smiling judiciously.

"Well?" Sendes asked her.

Sonja tilted her head, scratched her hair. "That's pretty good throwing, Sendes. The best you've done tonight. I don't know if I can beat that."

"Oh, be a sport about it!" one of Sendes' friends called.

"Yes, be a sport about it," Sendes urged her. "At least take your last throw."

"I don't know," Sonja said. "Shall we just call it a draw?"

Onlookers laughed.

"No, no, no," Sendes replied, very serious. "Now, I've had a slow start when you were way ahead. You can't just throw away the game, now that I'm on the verge of winning. Be a sport. Take your last throw, and I'll charge you only one cup of beer for losing. How's that?"

Sonja shrugged, glanced at the bull's eye. "But how can I try for the bull's eye when your knife is in the way?" she protested.

"Oh, very well," Sendes acquiesced. "I'll remove it."

He made a step in that direction, but a companion

held him back. "No, no, no, no! Rules is rules! The knife stays where it stuck." He looked, scowling, at Sonja.

Sonja shook her head. "Very well. I guess I'll just take my last throw and let that be the end of it."

"That's a sport." Sendes smiled, sipping again from his cup.

She was lithe and graceful as she moved forward, with all the smooth coordination of a jungle cat. Her hair fell in deep scarlet waves down her back. Dressed as she was in mail armor, she had seemed an affront to many a proud male in the tavern that night; and no matter how much she had drunk with them, or how well she had thrown, many had looked upon it as a presumption, or some sort of rude jest. A woman in warrior's armor, drinking and throwing knives with men! Well, she'd laughed and drunk and jested and thrown all night, and had even had some luck, but now she was finally going to have her bottle uncorked when Sendes won the bull's eye contest—

She moved with such ease and litheness that she took her small audience by surprise. There was no pause, no display of histrionics. In one fluid movement she had leaned forward, pulled her knife from its sheath at her waist, stepped to the line and pivoted. The weapon flashed in a blur; wood splintered and metal sang before anyone there had expected the knife to reach the wall.

Sonja smiled and glanced around. Sendes, astonished, dropped his cup.

"Damn me to the Hells!" called out one of his friends.

Her knife had driven home squarely in the bull's eye, cutting straight through Sendes'. The wooden handle of the Corinthian's weapon was split in two—no mean feat, for it was of hard wood imported from Kush—and the metal blade was scarred deeply where Sonja's had slid alongside it.

Sendes ran to the wall, pulled out Sonja's knife and stared at his own ruined weapon. "Impossible," he breathed.

Sonja walked up to him, smiling. "Have that back?"

Numbly, Sendes let her take the knife. She sheathed it. Sendes shook his head. "Impossible," he breathed again.

"I'll let you pass on the beer," said Sonja, grinning at him. "I think you're going to need your money to buy a new knife."

Silence—astounded silence—and then, in a burst, wild cheers, guffaws, whistles. Sendes' men crowded forward to clap Sonja on the back and offer her drinks.

They sat at their table and laughed. When Sendes came over, Sonja apologized. "I tried to tell you," she purred. "I didn't really think it would happen quite that way."

"Like hell," Sendes growled.

"Oh, cheer up!" urged one of his friends. "It was worth that damned knife to see a throw like that!" Turning to Sonja: "Where did you ever learn to do it? It's remarkable!"

Sonja gestured negatingly. "I wear my armor for a purpose," she said. "I am a free sword, a swordswoman; don't you think it wise for one who wears weapons to know how to use them? I've led many lives—" She stopped speaking, then said no more —feeling, perhaps, that she had said too much already.

Glancing at Sendes, she seemed about to make another comment to him—but saw that Sendes was staring past her, looking toward the center of the tavern. As she and the others at the table turned, too, following his gaze, Sonja became aware of a growing silence in the room.

In the center of the tavern was a young woman—tall, dark-haired, dressed in extremely fine clothes and sporting jewelries that marked her as no common inhabitant of this side of town. Yet Sonja got the impression that many of the people in the tavern did, indeed, know her. Certainly Sendes appeared to. He went so far as to stand up and hold out a hand, indicating to the young woman that she should come to the table. She advanced.

As Sonja stared, measuring the woman up and down, the man sitting next to her at the table—a burly man with a big, hairy belly spilling out over his sword-belt—leaned forward and whispered in Sonja's ear: "Endithor's daughter."

Sonja's brows raised.

"Areel," Sendes greeted the woman. He pushed back his chair and reached to get one for her from a neighboring table.

But Areel held up a hand. "I would like to speak with you alone, Sendes, if I might."

Those at the table took the hint. They all stood up, quaffed the last of their cups, straightened belts and swords and bade good-night to Sendes. One or two, perhaps on more familiar terms with Areel, offered her expressions of condolence on her father's death. She accepted these with a proudly raised chin.

Sonja was the last to go. She lingered, watching Sendes, watching Areel. Areel—proud, aloof, with deep black eyes full of intelligence and purpose—lent Sonja a slow gaze. Both women stared at one another for what seemed a long moment, but no word was spoken between them.

Sonja walked off. "Good-night to you, Sendes."

"Good-night, Red Sonja."

"We'll throw again, sometime."

"Yes, all right. Yes." He seemed a bit flustered; he smiled nervously at Sonja, then stepped behind Areel to pull out a chair for her.

Sonja walked away, pestered with thoughts. As she crossed the tavern one of Sendes' companions, the burly one, gestured to her. "Have another cup with us?"

"No, I think not. It's getting late."

"Have you some important engagement?"

"No."

"Sit a moment."

Curious, Sonja complied; as she sat down, she shot another glance back at Sendes and Areel, who were huddled at their shadowed table paying no attention to anyone else.

"You just met Sendes tonight, did you not?" asked the burly man.

"Yes. What of it?" said Sonja, perplexed.

The man shrugged. "It's strange." He looked back at the table. "I don't like it."

Sonja asked: "Isn't that the daughter of the noble-man who was killed today?"

"Aye. . . ."

"What's she doing with Sendes?"

The man's dark eyes looked into hers. "They've known each other for a time. Sendes never said so, but I think they were lovers, once. He served as a guard at the palace for a time. I think that's where they met."

"What's sinister in that?"

"Nothing. But now he's employed by Count Nalor."

"So who is Nalor?" asked Sonja.

A grim smile, skewed. "Only the most powerful man in the city. He's a ruthless bastard—controls all the politics and all the politicians. Sendes doesn't like him, but he pays well for good private soldiers, and I don't think Sendes could make better money anywhere else."

Sonja was becoming impatient. "So what does it all matter?"

"To you, maybe it doesn't. I guess you're not involved, except that you know Sendes. But—with Endithor executed. . . . You see, he was a councillor, and Nalor is a councillor. For Endithor to have been killed in public, Nalor would have had to arrest him and sign all the papers. I don't know all the details; but knowing what I do about Nalor, I'd bet a gold pin that Areel suspects something funny is going on. And since she knows Sendes, and since Sendes works for Nalor. . . ." He dropped open hands on the table.

"You may be letting your imagination run away with you," Sonja told him.

"I hope so. I like Sendes. I don't get to see him that often—I pass through Shadizar only a few times a year. I'm with the caravan that pulled in this morning; I'm leaving tomorrow morning. Hopefully I'll see Sendes alive when I return. I look forward to his company when I'm here, and I don't want anything to happen to him."

Sonja stood up. "He'll be all right. He can take care of himself. You're just worried because it's late and you're tired."

"I hope you're right, Red Sonja."

"Take care—" She laughed. "I've forgotten your name. Too many names and faces for one night, in this place."

"Bear Gut." He extended his hand.

"That's right." She smiled at him; big, hairy belly, so his friends called him Bear Gut. "Good-night, Bear Gut."

"Good-night, Sonja."

They shook hands, and Sonja walked on through the tavern. At the door, going out, she took a last glance back at Sendes and Areel. Something, some uneasiness she could not define, prickled her consciousness. Then she went out.

The night was warm but not muggy. From near and far came the sounds of ribaldry and carousing, for Shadizar came to life after daylight had fled and remained lively till its return. As Sonja walked briskly to her apartment quarters several blocks away, she was alert but not overly concerned for her own safety. Shadizar the Wicked, though a crossroads for all the thieves, murderers, pimps, rogues and renegades of the world, had yet its own sense of protocol. Variety was so common, crime and retribution so frequent, and vice so unnoticed that the figure of a red-haired swordswoman making her way down the streets, passing beneath the torches and oil lamps of various establishments, did not provoke the attention it might have in other places.

Besides, Red Sonja knew how to defend herself—and her best defense, she knew, was her own natural walk, sure and confident, plus her mail shirt and the longsword that swung at her hip. In Shadizar, as everywhere else, the strong preyed upon the weak, and Sonja knew the city as well as she knew herself. Only the most drunken, mad or desperate would dare risk death or disfigurement to gain the few coins a lone sword-bearer might be presumed to carry.

The safest route to Sonja's roominghouse was around the farther block and one street over, where the main avenues were somewhat lit with lamps and torches, and where late-comers still passed by or loitered. But the quickest route was through the alley just ahead of her. It was a short passage, wholly unlit, through the garbage and clutter between two tall, old brick buildings. Without hesitation, second thoughts or precautions (save for a reflexive right hand on her sword pommel), Sonja swung down the alley.

She heard squeaks and scamperings ahead of her—rats in the garbage. A few pairs of yellow and red eyes slid low to the ground, moving away before her advance. A small breeze trapped by the alley fluttered on scraps of paper; the distant light of oil lamps glinted now and then on broken pieces of glass.

Half-way down on the alley, Sonja heard another noise —a brief cough or a low whisper. She neither hastened nor slowed her pace, but instinctively her fingers gripped her sheathed sword more tightly. Her eyes cast about; she listened for more noise between the sounds of her own footfalls on the litter.

Another noise—slight, but there—and a movement of a shadow. Aye, before her, and behind her. Sonja's nostrils flared; she smiled slightly in tense anticipation. If they—whoever they might be—tried to attack her for her purse, chances were that her own purse would be heavier following the encounter.

She took a breath, slowed her pace just a little—and then the voices rang out.

"We've got her!"—from in front.

"Get her!"—from behind.

"Hurry! Now!"—from the front again, only a different voice.

And: "At her, Chost!"—a second voice from behind.

Sonja snarled as shadows leaped at her. She threw herself back against the wall of the alley and her sword hissed from its sheath like a rearing cobra, flashing an arc of caught torchlight in the center of the darkness.

Chapter 2.

At the sound of the sword, the shadows held back. Sonja braced herself, legs wide, boots clamped to the earth of the alley. Quickly, with her free left hand, she whipped out her dagger. Depending more on her ears than her eyes, she judged the advancement and cautious waiting on both sides of her. She breathed as quietly as she could; she listened; she watched.

Faint footfalls. No more voices. Then:

"She's got a sword!" came a cautious whisper.

The shadows did not advance.

Something puzzled Sonja: something in the tone of the voices that had called out. Looking both to left and right, she tried to discern the exact positions of her attackers as best she could.

The moments lingered and drew out, with the shadows holding back, indecisive. Four against one—and yet the shadows lingered. Sonja, nerves tingling, blood racing, senses all heightened and alert, finally demanded action.

"Come ahead, damn you!" she growled. "Who's first? Come ahead!"

As though answering her taunt, one of the figures to her left seemed to advance a pace. Instantly Sonja responded, swinging her sword out in a wide arc before her, ducking almost to a crouch as she pivoted across the alley and backed herself against the opposite wall.

The sudden, swift movement took her would-be attackers by surprise. The nearest yelped—though Sonja could tell that her blade had met no resistance—and scampered away; running, he stumbled into his partner at that end of the alley. Then Sonja saw, peripherally, both figures take to their heels and vanish into the farther avenue. Betraying torches showed them to be very small men, thin and almost elvish in the shadows.

Her right flank clear, Sonja turned to her left. The two shadows still hovered, dimly outlined against the distant oil lamps beyond. The one farthest from her, panicking, cried out: "Chost, it's no good!" and ran off.

So one remained, standing there, uncertain whether to run off and chance a sword in the back, or stay and—fight? Beg?

Sonja jumped ahead, sword pointed for the ruffian—

And the figure moved, instinctively reacting by throwing himself backwards, half-turning and attempting to run.

Sonja gave chase. In a moment she had gobbled up the space between them. As the small figure broke out of the alley into the street, Sonja whacked him on the buttocks with the flat of her sword. The would-be robber howled and went flying, knocked to his hands and knees.

"Don't—!" He cringed with anticipation.

Sonja stepped boldly to him, dropped her sword-point to the side of his throat. "Don't move!"

Ragged, hoarse breathing, as of one fear-gripped, answered her. She returned her side-knife to its sheath, then took her time looking over her assailant—

And smiled, doubtfully. The lad was—how old?

Maybe eleven, twelve seasons. Twelve full years. Sonja shook her head ruefully, pulled back her blade, slapped the boy once more on the buttocks.

"Now stand up! Don't try to run away or I *will* stab you through. Understand?"

"Gods, yes!"

"Stand up, urchin."

Terrified, the youngster got to his feet, eyes fixed on Sonja's sword.

"Now, what was the idea of that back there?"

The lad did not answer.

"Tell me! Look at me, damn it!"

Wide eyes met hers.

"What were you and your friends trying to do, hey? Is that the way you spend your nights? Trying to rob innocent people?"

In the dim light, she saw a slow change spread over the boy's face. With the threat of death gone, with a chance now for talk and bargaining, his expression became harder. Gone was the terrified boy's look; in its place came a street-wise arrogance, a narrowing of the eyes, a calculating appraisal of this tall, red-haired woman. She wasn't going to kill him. No, she didn't want that kind of trouble. Whoever she was, this woman with a sword, she wasn't a murderer—so why should he answer her questions? All he had to do was wait till she relaxed some more, then run off. She wouldn't give chase; she didn't want the trouble. And once he got away—gods, but he'd find those other three and soundly beat their heads against the brick for leaving him in the lurch like this!

Sonja read the lad's expression as surely as if she herself were twelve again, and poor, and in need of food and money.

"Don't care to tell me, heh?"

The sword dropped some more.

"Well. . . ."

The boy's thin legs shuddered, preparing to run.

"Don't, damn it!" Sonja yelled, raising the sword again to his throat.

He yelped. The pressure of the point forced him to stagger back; he nearly tripped, then walked backwards quickly to the alley wall, where Sonja held him pinned with the point tickling his throat.

"Now, tell me!" she hissed. "You think I'm just going to let you run away, after pulling a stunt like that?"

"G-g-godsss. . . !" he gurgled.

"What you did wasn't too smart," Sonja told him. "What the hell made you and your friends try it?"

Gone, again, was the street-wise arrogance; back, once more, were the trembling legs, the terrified eyes and the sweating pallor.

"Was it for excitement?" Sonja asked him. "You're a little young to risk getting carved up, just looking for excitement. Money? Did you think you needed money to impress your girlfriend? Was that it? Hey?"

The boy swallowed, shook his pale hair, looked up into Sonja's eyes. "Food," he told her.

"Food?" she muttered aloud. Immediately she saw it, and realized she should have known it earlier. She recognized it all: the thin face, the pale skin, the thin arms hidden beneath the ragged sleeves. She had too often been hungry herself, and had stolen out of desperation as well, not to recognize that the boy was telling the truth.

"What's your name, lad?"

From between trembling lips: "Chost."

"And you were trying to steal my money to buy food?"

He bobbed his head—carefully, so as not to impale himself on Sonja's sword.

"Don't you have any parents?"

"No."

"Where do you live?"

He swallowed thickly. "I don't know. . . ."

"In the alleys?"

"I guess. . . ."

Sonja shook her head. No, there was no point in killing him. He was no threat. But it wouldn't do to—

She reached for her pouch, tugged it from her belt, thumbed it open and spilled four coins onto the alley floor: two coppers, a silver minar and a gold piece—a lot of money for back alleys. She returned her purse to her belt, pulled back the sword.

"Take the money, Chost."

"What?"

"Take the money."

"N-no. You'll stab me."

"In Mitra's name! Will you just reach down and take the damned money?"

Timidly, he did so, watching Sonja's sword. He dropped to his knees, not quite in control of his legs, gathered up the coins and held them tightly in his white hands. Then he stood up, facing Sonja.

"You're not going to kill me?"

"No, I'm not going to kill you."

"You're not going to call the city patrol?"

"No, I'm not. But—you listen to me, now. You take that money and buy food for yourself and your friends, understand? Don't gamble it or let anyone else steal it from you. You understand?"

"Gods, yes!"

"And one thing more, Chost. Tell your friends not to try to attack me again, or next time I *will* get someone through the belly. Understand?"

His head bobbed up and down.

"All right, go on, now. Wait a minute."

Chost hovered, uncertain.

"If you just *have* to take on someone with a sword in order to eat, do it right, will you? Throw some rocks to make noise—that gets most people confused—and get a blanket or something to throw on them. You can't fight what you can't see. Plan it better, all right?"

"I—All right. All right."

"How the hell do you expect to survive for very long, if you act like a jackass?"

"I—I don't know."

Sonja hid a smile. "Go on. Get out of here."

The lad nodded quickly, half-turned and started to run, pivoted and looked back.

Sonja dropped her sword into its sheath; it slid home with a clank.

Chost took off, running, his thin boots slapping on the cobbles.

Sonja sighed, wiped her nose. Kids. Shadizar hadn't changed—no better, but not much worse. She wondered whether it were better for the city to spend tax monies helping these urchins, as was done in some other communities, or just letting them run wild to learn how to survive. The lot of such children was not good, no matter what the system.

But it was none of her affair. She, herself, had run wild and learned to survive—though at not *quite* such a tender age. . . .

She exited the alley and continued on in the direction she had started. There were no more scampering noises, no more tribes of young lads trying to jump her for her purse. From the alley she crossed a street and walked toward her boarding house.

Pushing through the old wooden door, she went up

two flights of stairs in the musty darkness and into her room on the highest floor of the house. She closed the door and bolted it, undressed in the darkness, stuck her sword into the floor beside the bed so that it stood ready to hand, then crawled under the covers, sank back and quickly fell asleep.

Outside in the night, many streets away, Chost finally found his friends, cursed them for running off on him, and showed them the money he'd gotten.

"She *gave* it to me," he told them.

"Did you see where she went?" they asked, staring at the coins.

"Aye," Chost answered, jangling the money thoughtfully in his hands. "I saw where she lives. . . ."

Shadizar in the morning was a necropolis, where the ghosts of night returned indoors to hide from the sunlight. The living of the day awakened slowly to pursue their business, ignorant of, or ignoring, the night-phantoms and night-lives existing side-by-side with them.

Sonja awoke late; it was almost noon when she threw back her covers, stretched her long arms and legs, yawned and shook her head. The wine from last night tasted bad in her mouth. She lay for a moment in the bed, its uncomfortable old cushions itching her back, and listened to the street sounds. From outside the door came sounds from elsewhere in the ancient rooming-house: coughs, yells, a dish breaking.

She got up and washed herself with the water on the stand in the corner, promising herself that today she would finally get to the public baths and loll for a good long time in the pool. She dressed, combed out her long hair with the silver comb she carried in her boot, then strapped on her sword. Opening her window to let the room air out, she left the place and clomped downstairs.

Meals were being served in the tavern. Sonja took a table and ordered lunch, ate it and wondered what she would do with her day. Her only reason for being in Shadizar was that she had by chance and adventure been pointed in Shadizar's direction. She knew people, or at least knew the names of some persons, in the city; she could inquire after them. Money she was not presently in desperate need of; but sooner or later she would have to earn some more, one way or another. It wouldn't hurt to check some of the public notices in the square for positions needing to be filled— announcements of caravans or expeditions needing swordsmen and soldiers, or such like. It might happen that she would overhear some rumor in a tavern, or even meet up with an old acquaintance or two. Many paths were known to cross in the city of Shadizar.

Sonja finished her meal, paid the master of the house and sauntered out. Two streets over were the public stables where she had settled her horse; she went there to check up on it, was pleased to find it well-fed and watered, and made sure the stable groom understood that the stallion was to be exercised twice a day. The groom assured her that such was the stable's policy, but Sonja dropped him a few extra coppers to make sure. It wouldn't do to have her horse "stolen" and sold to the next caravan out of town.

The day was bright and hot, for it was early summer. Sonja was warm in her mail. Walking leisurely, she headed for the main square, pausing along the way to look at goods in shops, or loiter to talk with other passers-by, or occasionally return obscene gestures to knaves who whistled at her figure, cat-called or made rude comments about this or that portion of her anatomy.

Following one altercation with an offensive

lout—"Hey, Red, if you need help carrying those, I got two good hands!" "Come and try it, you serpent's son, and you'll walk home with the wind whistling between your legs!"—Sonja at first ignored her name being called out in the middle of a street heavy with traffic. But as the voice persisted, she turned on her heel, snarl ready—only to see that it was Sendes, waving to her from a large open litter.

"Come over here!" he called.

Sonja smirked self-derisively and pushed through the people to get to him.

"What good luck to find you!" Sendes exclaimed. "What are you doing today?"

"Seeing the sights."

"Have you any plans for this evening?"

"None in particular. What did you have in mind, Sendes? Another go at the knife?"

He laughed out loud. "No, no, no. Far better entertainment than that. Hop in, I'll tell you about it."

He opened more widely the curtains of the litter and Sonja got in. Sendes called to his bearers, four in front, four behind, and they hoisted the poles to their shoulders and started off down the street again.

The ride was bumpy and noisy. Sonja was mildly impressed by the obvious wealth displayed by the interior of the conveyance. It was large enough to hold two or three persons, and its coverings were of silk, its ornaments of jade and ivory and gold, its pillows and cushions brocaded with the finest skill of Eastern weavers.

"How did you manage all this?" Sonja asked. "Beat a rich man at the bull's eye?"

Again Sendes laughed. "No, I'm afraid not. This thing isn't mine, though I wish it were. No, it belongs to Lord Count Nalor."

"Oh."

"Ever hear of him?"

"In passing, I think."

"He's a very rich and very influential politician here in Shadizar. He hired me as one of his guardsmen a little over a year ago. It certainly is an easy life."

"So I see."

"You know. . . ." Sendes leaned closer. "If you like, Sonja, I could put in a good word for you, to Nalor. He can always use good protection, and the idea of a female soldier would probably appeal to him." He raised his eyebrows questioningly.

"No doubt," Sonja agreed thoughtfully. "Thanks, Sendes—but it doesn't appeal to me."

"Ah, well. In any event, that wasn't why I picked you up. You see, Nalor's giving a feast tonight, and I thought you might like to come along."

"A feast?"

"Yes. He's invited all sorts of people. It'll be very amusing. He does this every few months—entertains all the politicians and councillors and what-not he has in his pocket."

"I doubt I'd fit in very well."

"Maybe not, but I'm sure you'd like it! Nalor makes a point of inviting interesting people."

"So I'd be a show piece, eh?"

Sendes chuckled. "No, no, not at all. But it's a free meal—good food—some entertainment. You've just gotten into town, so Nalor might be interested in some of your opinions about outside affairs. You understand."

"Maybe he'll want to hire me as a spy or an informant, you mean?"

Sendes laughed again, mellowly. "No, I doubt it. But I think if you come along, you'll enjoy it."

"Are you on your way there now?"

"Sort of. Nalor asked me to purchase a few things for tonight."

"Doesn't he have servants to do that?"

"Oh, certainly. But I volunteered. Gets me off work for a day, out into the sunshine, around the city."

"I see."

"What do you say? Care to come along?"

Sonja shrugged. "For a free meal, sure. Why not? Only—I don't understand why you don't invite your girlfriend."

"My girlfriend?" Sendes was puzzled.

Sonja said: "That young woman in the tavern last night."

Sendes' expression altered quickly; he looked away. "She's not a girlfriend."

"Areel—wasn't that her name?"

"A passing acquaintance, that's all."

The litter jounced on for a few moments. Sonja asked: "Wasn't that her father who was executed yesterday?"

Now Sendes eyed her sharply. He gripped Sonja's hand strongly; the strength of his grip and the light in his eyes implied a warning. "Don't mention that, Sonja."

"Why not?"

"Don't mention it ever again. Not to me, not in front of Nalor or his servants. All right? Especially not in front of Nalor."

"Let go of my hand, Sendes, or you'll lose those fingers."

Startled by the cool control of her voice, he let her go.

"Sorry. Forgive my rudeness. But—I mean it! Don't mention that, ever again."

"And why not?"

Sendes looked away once more. Puzzled, Sonja studied him. Finally he said, in a low tone: "You are aware that there are such things as sorcerers and evil magic?"

Sonja hid a terse smile. "Oh, vaguely. I've heard such things exist."

Sendes faced her again, pain in his eyes. "Areel's father—Count Endithor—He was an enemy of Nalor's. They fought bitterly in Council for many years. That was public knowledge. What is *not* public knowledge is that Endithor tried, two nights ago, to slay Nalor by using black magic."

"Indeed?"

"It is true. And that was the real reason for the execution."

"Endithor must have been a very evil man."

Sendes shook his head. "That's the surprising thing. He was not evil. He was a good man, devoted to Areel, his only daughter. I can't understand what would make him try such a thing."

Sonja could think of no answer.

"Anyway," Sendes went on, "I think that's part of Nalor's reason for having this fete tonight—to put the memory of that behind everyone."

"Nalor himself," said Sonja, "is not an especially guiltless person, Sendes—or so I've heard."

"What do you mean by that?"

"I mean, the gaining of power always brings the loss of many other things—don't you think?"

He watched her carefully for a moment, then looked past her, out between the partly-opened curtains of the litter. Suddenly he leaned out his side and called for his bearers to halt. There was a series of shudders as the big men slowed their pace, lifted the carrying-poles off their shoulders, rested the conveyance on the ground.

"It almost slipped my mind," Sendes told Sonja, opening the curtains on his side of the palanquin. "There are a few more things I must order here at the market-place for Lord Nalor. Come on. Once we're done with that, we can head to his apartments. All right?"

Lord Count Nalor's quarters took up the entire first floor of one wing of the stately apartment house located not far from Shadizar's palace. Home to the preeminent councillors and nobles of the city, the house and its grounds showed in every detail the artful sumptuousness enjoyed by Zamoran aristocracy: marble friezes and columns, inlays of bronze and gold, silver and ivory, jade and jet. Silken tapestries—lush gardens with huge, rushing fountains—animals and birds, caged or running free—slaves and servants of every size and color, responsible for every duty imaginable: all this attested to the overwhelming wealth of Shadizar's aristocracy.

Sonja and Sendes arrived late in the afternoon, as the sun was just touching the tips of the tallest trees to the west. If Sendes had hoped that Sonja might be overwhelmed by the regal luxury of the apartment and the obvious high estate of Nalor's guests, he was disappointed; it was not in the Hyrkanian's nature to be awed by displays of wealth, nor to shrink in humility before opportunistic councillors, fat money-handlers or well-oiled politicians. For these, she well knew, lived a life of servility and submission every bit as demeaning, in its own way, as that of their underlings.

"Put us down here," Sendes ordered his bearers as the litter came abreast of a side entrance. "You can come with me, Sonja," he said as they stepped forth. "I must speak to Nalor's seneschal about the day's business."

On the way in, they saw the conveyances of many

autocrats and plutocrats passing by, on their way to the main entrance. Sendes, aware of his station in Nalor's employ, dutifully bowed his head and made respectful signs to these important personages. Sonja said nothing, moved not at all; there was even a scowl on her face.

Sendes noticed. He elbowed her. "Be pleasant to these people," he warned. "Smile and say hello. You're a foreigner—you don't have to make the sign of the gods—but if you act like you don't respect them, they'll be upset."

Her response was terse and uncompromising. "Good."

Another palanquin went by; a tanned fat man sporting a jeweled beard looked at them. Sendes nodded, smiled, lifted his hand with curled fingers—and sighed when he saw that Sonja still did not respond.

The bearers, having set down the litter, had formed into a line. Sendes beckoned and led the way into the side entrance. It led into the kitchen, a huge room swarming with slaves carrying large plates loaded with foods and goblets. Sonja felt suddenly hungry as the delicious odors of fine cooking came to her.

"That's Imf, the seneschal," commented Sendes, pointing out a man dressed in a fine, gold-colored tunic and white-and-purple sandals. This worthy seemed harried, and was throwing out orders in all directions at once.

"Through the west door!" he bawled lispingly to three naked slave girls. "No, no, the *west* door! Where do they *raise* such stupid things? You, Sodos!—lead those boys past the curtains. And make sure that *every*one has a pitcher of wine next to him, do you understand? Girls! Through *that* door! Goodness of the gods!" Imf stamped his feet in desperation. "Were you all born without *ears?*"

Sendes made his way through the rushing bodies, Sonja following, and tried to get the seneschal's attention. "Imf! Imf! *Imf!*"

"Oh, Sendes, what *is* it? Can't you see I'm *busy?*"

Sendes produced a roll of parchment. "This is the list of what was ordered today. It should all have been delivered this afternoon, Imf."

"Just tuck it down my trousers. You, there—wait with those appetizers! Take *those* trays first, will you? Oh, goodness, goodness!"

Sendes wiped his nose, glanced at Sonja, tapped the rolled parchment against one arm.

"Imf?"

"Through the *curtains,* you bovine mistake of the gods!"

"Imf?"

"Oh, in a moment, Sendes. No—no, Hedos! That line of trays goes—"

Exasperated, Sendes turned on his heel. A slave-girl was just passing by him, carrying a large tray on her shoulder loaded with diced meats, fruits and steaming vegetables. Without a pause Sendes plunged the rolled tube of parchment into the pile so that it stuck out awkwardly, stained and steaming, absurd.

"Sendes!" Imf cried in horror. "Sendes! What have you *done?*"

Sendes took Sonja's hand and pulled her through the milling kitchen-crowd, calling after him: "Just make sure you pay those bills, Imf!"

"Stop, wench!" they heard Imf bawl. "Oh, curse it! I *need* that paper!"

Sonja was laughing as she and Sendes exited the kitchen and went down a long corridor. "That wasn't nice," she said. "The poor bastard is up to his ears in it back there."

"Oh," Sendes mimicked, "tho it wathn't nithe, was it? Well, if he isn't used to it by now, he never will be. He must like it, or he wouldn't ask for it. Damned fool!"

The corridor led into a large foyer, where the last of a long line of well-dressed nobles were just passing into the main feasting hall. Lord Nalor stood, with servants, at the open portals, smiling and greeting each of his guests with a firm handshake and a jest or comment. Sendes led Sonja to a column, apart from the guests, telling her they'd wait a moment until the greetings were done with.

Sonja leaned against the pillar and crossed her arms. "So that's him, huh?"

"Aye, that's Nalor."

"He just oozes it, doesn't he?"

"What?"

She looked at Sendes knowingly.

"Well," Sendes said apologetically, "he pays well."

"I'm sure. I'm sure he does. Why don't you give at least some of it back to the people in the streets? They're the ones who need it—and probably the ones who supply most of it."

He did not reply, only gave her a glance that implied he doubted her good taste if not her sanity. Then, seeing that the last guest was just entering the feasting hall, Sendes moved ahead, motioning for Sonja to follow. Nalor turned at the sight of his guardsman, opened his hands towards him.

"Ah, Sendes. Did everything go well this afternoon?"

"Aye, my lord. I trust all that I ordered arrived safely?"

"I imagine so." Nalor nodded. "We'll have to speak with Imf about that. Who is your guest, Sendes?" His eyes settled on Sonja, approvingly.

"Her name is Red Sonja, my lord. She beat me at points last night."

"So?" Nalor chortled. "You're a warrior for hire, I take it, Red Sonja?"

"Aye." Her eyes settled on Nalor, disapprovingly.

"But not Zamoran, I take it?"

"Hyrkanian, Lord Nalor."

"Ah, I see." Things had not always been well between Zamora and Hyrkania. "Well, you are welcome, in any event, as a friend of my young guardsman, here. I value Sendes like a son. Won't you please come in? Enjoy your evening, and perhaps we shall converse more later."

"Thank you, Lord Nalor." Sonja strode past him into the hall, uncomfortably aware of his gaze following her. Sendes came in just behind her; as he passed Nalor, Sonja heard the Councillor whisper in his ear:

"The far wall, Sendes. A swordswoman? Gods!"

Sendes blushed sheepishly and hastened his pace, indicating to Sonja a low table at the far end of the hall, away from the nobles and gathered councillors.

The sun went down, the last of its reflected light in the huge hall dimming and graying and vanishing, replaced by torches and great oil lamps lighted by slaves. The food was distributed and replaced in never-ending cycles; Sonja ate until she felt she would burst, and then continued to sample morsels of this or that culinary delectable. "Can I take some of this with me?" she asked Sendes at one point. "I haven't had food like this in an age!" He laughed.

The entertainments provided met with resounding approval all around. There were dancers, singly and in troupes—singers and musicians—a masque performed by a hired band of travelling actors and actresses—even six brawny acrobats taking turns at fighting a deadly Cimmerian bear, imported by Nalor especially for the occasion. A ring of well-armed guards protected the banqueting spectators from any possible harm, should the bear in its frenzy go amok; and the greatest applause of the evening met the six acrobats when, en masse, they finally attacked the bear for the kill. Only one of the men was severely wounded, and Nalor's physician assured the audience that he would certainly survive once his arm was amputated.

Sonja was angered at that spectacle. "Not especially on account of the acrobats," she told Sendes, "—if they're fools enough to perform in Nalor's house, they all deserve to be mauled. I'm mad for the bear's sake."

"The bear?" Sendes asked her, astonished.

"Certainly," Sonja told him. "It wasn't the poor brute's choice to be dragged here so that gawking weaklings could have their satisfaction watching him tormented and killed—from a safe distance, of course. They like to see blood flowing, when it isn't their own—but put any one of these flabby gawkers into the bear's den, and see whose blood quickly flows!"

"But that's missing the point," Sendes patiently explained. "It's merely an entertainment."

"Aye—for these overfed bureaucrats," Sonja replied, "but not for the bear. No. No. Put them in the forest with the bear, Sendes, and see who is entertained. That would be entertainment more to my taste, I think!"

Sendes shook his head, not understanding her; but, aware that she was a primitive far from home and in many ways a stranger to civilization, he poured her another goblet of wine, smiled apologetically to any nearby who might have overheard, and turned the conversation into other channels.

The slaying of the Cimmerian bear was not the end to Nalor's surprise diversions. As the carcass was dragged away, the Lord Count rose from his table and advanced to the center of the hall, being careful not to step in any of the blood. Then, lifting his hands for silence, he announced:

"My friends! My friends! It is now my great good pleasure to introduce to you, as the climax of tonight's festivities, the marvellous talents of a man some of you may already know. He is a dear and close friend of mine, a true scholar, a man of wisdom, learned in so many wondrous things that I could spend the rest of tonight and tomorrow detailing his many accomplishments and skills. But rather than bore you with such a lecture, I would have you be entertained and startled and amazed. So, let me now introduce to you my good friend, the practitioner of arcane arts and the master of many illusions, the outstanding magician, Lord Kus!"

Nalor clapped his hands; after a moment more applause sounded, but nothing resounding to fill up the hall. Too many in the audience, it seemed, were all too familiar with Count Nalor's good friend.

Sonja squirmed in her seat, hunching forward. Sendes sipped wine.

Nalor quickly returned to his table. For a long moment, the echo of his promise hung in the air. His introduction was met with no appearance by Lord Kus. Voices began to murmur.

Then came an explosion—a flash of fire in the center of the hall. Nobles gasped; slave-girls, astonished and taken by surprise, dropped their trays and squealed; dishes and goblets clattered.

As the burst of fire in the hall flared upward and vanished, as the smoke cleared away, there stood boldly before Nalor's guests the tall, dark-robed, sinister figure of Kus.

Acting the showman. Pretending to the art of the travelling miracle-doer, thought Sonja—even as she somehow immediately sensed that he was more than that. . . .

Kus bowed gracefully to his stunned audience, looked down and noticed the bear's blood on the floor. "I see," he said, "that my host's servants have been remiss in their duties. No matter. I would be pleased to help them in their toil."

With a sweep of his hand the bear's blood shimmered and burst into a glowing flame—an unreal flame, burning in blues and greens. In a moment it was burnt out, gone—as was the bear's blood. No crimson remained on the tiles of the floor, neither was there any stain or char from the weird flame.

Kus bowed to the scant applause; Nalor's claps sounded the loudest.

"A few small tricks," Kus assured the ringing faces, "to pay beforehand for my meal. Have I any volunteers to aid me in my demonstrations?"

None assented.

Kus laughed. "Perhaps one of my lord's young servants. . . . ?"

"Yes, yes!" Nalor cried out, and took hold of a young slave-girl by the arm.

"My lord," she protested, "I would rather not have to—"

"Come, come," Nalor urged her in a cold tone. "You won't be harmed." Rudely he pushed her around the table, slapped her on the buttocks so that she scampered out onto the floor.

She stood there timidly, clad only in a brief loincloth and sandals. Kus regarded her appreciatively. "Come, come," he purred. "You're not afraid, are you?"

The girl shuddered and shivered, saying something that could not be overheard. But, afraid of Nalor, she came closer.

"You're a timid thing, aren't you?" Kus smiled. "Perhaps you would not be so timid if you were more like a tigress?"

The girl didn't say anything.

"Perhaps I should help you?" Kus inquired. Without warning he spread his hands and ran one along the girl's back, the other along her front, blurring them so quickly that what he did could not be seen. In a moment, he stepped back. Gasps of astonishment rose in the hall.

The girl looked down at herself—and cried out. Upon her bare skin, from neck to knees, there had appeared strange stripes: brown lines, furry, of actual hair, running crosswise upon her thighs and belly, breasts and back.

"What do you think?" Kus called to his audience. "Is she not a tigress?"

Sonja grunted uneasily. Sendes looked at her. "What is it, Sonja?"

"Sorcery." Her voice was thick.

Sendes snorted. "Oh, come on. It's simply sleight-of-hand. I've seen people do things like this before."

Sonja shook her head. "My instincts are never wrong, Sendes. This may be illusion, but it isn't sleight-of-hand. It's sorcery."

The slave-girl whimpered and moaned.

"Not a tigress at heart, hey?" Kus frowned thoughtfully. "Perhaps a pale flower?" He gestured rapidly with both hands; in a moment the stripes had vanished, but the girl's pale hair had transformed into a bundle of wild-flowers.

Harsh laughter now sounded out around the room,

and Nalor's carried hugely.

The terrified slave-girl felt above her head and began to cry; she dropped to her knees, wailing and sobbing.

Kus shook his head. "How undignified. Not a wild-flower either, hey? Not much good for anything, are you? Very well—"

With another gesture the girl's natural hair was returned.

"Run along," Kus told her. "Let some kitchen boy comfort you in your tribulations."

The frightened girl ran off, sandals clattering on the stone, guffaws from the audience roaring behind her.

"I shall need a new subject, however," Kus now complained. "Perhaps. . . ?" He approached the long line of tables; his eyes scanned the participants. He came up to a grossly fat man, well-dressed, his neck and arms and belly glittering with costly jewels.

"Here's a good example," Kus declared, staring the fat man in the eyes. "Here's a well-made man—made of money, I suppose. Is that the case? Are you made of money?"

The fat man chortled gleefully. "You might say that!" he chuckled, slapping the table with his hands, looking around at his companions.

"I'll more than say it," Kus promised him. "I believe I can prove it. Here!" He reached across the table, spread his right hand into the fat man's greasy hair and began to rub. He rubbed quickly; the fat man's neck rolled this way and that. From his hair or from beneath Kus' hands—from somewhere—there flew dozens and dozens of Zamoran gold coins. They struck the faces of those next to the nobleman, clattered onto the table, dropped into plates of food and cups of drink.

Kus drew back. The fat man was dizzy, rolling in his seat with laughter. The pile of gold coins on the table before him brought peals of laughter from deep in his belly.

"Now, who else?" Kus wondered aloud, surveying the room. His gaze lingered on Nalor's and Nalor flashed a look at the other end of the room. Kus strode in that direction. His dark eyes fixed upon Sendes and Sonja.

"Now, who else?" he called out again.

Sonja tensed. Sendes noticed it, noticed how the Hyrkanian's sapphire eyes flashed as they met Kus' and suddenly knew that the sorcerer had decided upon her.

"By Mitra," she muttered, "if he dares to—!"

Sendes touched her shoulder. "Sonja, it's only a game."

Kus approached the table. "Here we are!" he announced. "Look at this flame-haired woman! What an attractive woman! And, as I say, flame-haired. Is your hair truly of flame, young woman, or is it—?"

Sonja leaped up, kicking back her chair; it smashed against the wall several arm-lengths behind. Sendes, startled, let out a hoarse cry. Kus instantly fell back a step.

Eyes glaring, nostrils flared, Sonja whipped out her sword and side-knife; her right foot was up against the table's edge, ready to kick the table at Kus if he made any move toward her.

"Try anything," Sonja yelled out, "and I'll drive steel through you! Do you understand, sorcerer?"

Nalor paled; he rose to his feet, sputtering.

A menacing glitter lit Kus' eyes.

"Sonja!" Sendes finally got out. "Don't you understand—?"

"Do you hear me, sorcerer?" she yelled out, ignoring Sendes, still glaring at Kus. "Make one move towards me, and I'll ram this sword through your black magician's heart!"

Chapter 3.

"Guards!" Lord Nalor bawled; *"Guards!* Take that woman!"

They moved forward from opposite corners of the hall, two lines of well-armored soldiers, spears held ready.

"Stand back!" Sonja called to them, without removing her eyes from Kus. "Stay back, you dogs, or more than bear's blood will stain this hall!"

They paused.

Nalor—white-faced, shivering with anger—sputtered with indignation. All around buzzed an ocean of comment: "Crazy woman!" "Savage!" "Woman who thinks she's a man—" "Must be out of her mind!" "Touched by the gods—" "Look how she handles that sword! I admire her spirit!" "Crazy woman. . . ."

Sendes stood up slowly, did not touch Sonja but whispered to her: "In the name of the gods, what are you doing? This isn't—!"

"Stay back!" Sonja called to Kus.

But the magician only removed himself another step or two, then leaned low in a mock bow, spread his arms, then brought his hands together as he straightened. "Patience, patience, flame-haired one," he murmured, eyes shimmering intensely. "You mistake me, young woman. I have no intention of harming you."

"I don't mistake you at all—sorcerer."

Kus smiled, turned to face Nalor. "Lord Count, obviously she has had a bit too much to drink, and my performances have put her on edge. I think it best that we defer any further entertainments for a while."

"I think it best," Nalor finally roared, "that this Hyrkanian wench be escorted from the hall and kicked out onto the street!"

Sonja glowered at him.

"Put up your sword, woman! Don't you know what it means to draw steel in someone's home?"

Sonja said nothing. There was hatred and defiance in her eyes.

Sendes seconded his master. "Please, Sonja, the threat is past. There never *was* a threat. Put away your steel, or he'll have you arrested."

Slowly, grudgingly, eyes still on Kus, she did so. She was trembling with energy; her face shone with perspiration; her eyes glared with anger and perhaps a touch of fear. "Don't you see what he is?" she muttered in a low voice to Sendes. "Mitra! Are all you people blinded?" Her blades settled noisily into their sheaths; she brought her leg down from the table-edge and stood straight and tall, the focus of all eyes in the room.

"Guards!" Nalor called. "Escort Sendes and his—his guest—from the hall! Now!" •

Sendes showed a sick face. "I might lose my job over this," he muttered to Sonja. He looked over at the guards, who were advancing. Sonja saw them; before they reached her, she pivoted and began exiting the hall herself. Past the rows of long tables she strode, past the many faces and eyes and gesturing hands of the guests.

The scowling gaze of Nalor followed her, and also a much darker, burning, more sinister pair of eyes.

She passed through the wide doors of the hall, strode boldly into the foyer. Without waiting for Sendes, she motioned for the servants there to open the portals and let her out.

Sendes followed—sheepish, humiliated, embarrassed. The guards let him go, but as he exited into the foyer Sendes heard a sound behind him, turned to see Nalor. The Councillor cornered him against a pillar.

"What was the purpose in bringing that barbarian here?"

"I—I don't know. She was amusing—lively. I thought you'd—"

"You thought wrong!"

"Forgive me," Sendes begged the hostile eyes. "I never suspected she was so quick-tempered, so quick with her sword."

To Sendes' surprise, Nalor showed a strange sort of smile. "It *was* exciting," he admitted. "She certainly took Kus aback." Then his face grew stern again. "But I'm trying to make a good impression upon these people, and I can't have barbarian women drawing swords among my guests!"

"I understand that."

"I hope that you do! She is never to come here again, is that understood?"

"Of course, Lord Nalor. But—?"

"But what?"

"Am I?"

"Are you what, Sendes?"

"To come here again? I mean—my job?"

Nalor scowled. "Your job is safe enough, for the time being. But I allow only one such mistake. You understand that, too, don't you?"

"Yes, of course, my lord. Of course."

"Now make sure that woman gets away from here without causing any more trouble. I don't want her trying any more stupid stunts on my grounds."

"Thank you, my lord."

"I expect to see you on duty tomorrow morning, Sendes. And we'll forget this ever happened."

"Thank you, Lord Nalor. Thank you."

"Now, go on."

Sendes hurried from the foyer, out the doors. Nalor watched him, his attitude shifting between quieted anger and a feeling of mirth. It *had* been a surprising, bizarre display, and that woman *had* put Kus in his place. Which was good. Anything that might keep Kus a bit off balance, and aware that he was not always in control of all situations, was to the good.

He turned, motioned to his guards, and re-entered the feasting hall. As he resumed his seat, he looked in vain for his magician.

"Kus has retired," a woman next to Nalor informed him. "He said he would return later for his meal. I believe he was a bit angry."

"Outfaced!" laughed someone else nearby. "Excellent entertainment, Lord Count!"

Nalor swallowed a deep slow breath, refrained from smiling, and reached for his wine cup.

Sonja was not outside. Sendes became concerned; he searched the street in both directions along the front of the apartment, but did not see her. For a moment he worried about the worst. But it was possible—and made more sense—that Sonja had probably just headed home.

Sendes went around to where slaves were loitering, drinking their own wine and jesting while they polished the palanquins and carriages. At a snap of his fingers four men strode up to him. "Find me a litter," he ordered them.

A few moments later he was being carried down the street, back in the direction from which he and Sonja had come earlier. For some time he looked in vain for her, until at last he noticed a tall woman in silvery mail exiting a tavern. Beneath the intermittent oil lamps her hair showed long and flame-red.

"Sonja!" Sendes called out.

Sonja looked back.

Sendes ordered his bearers to halt. Sonja walked on.

"Sonja, stop a moment!" Sendes jumped from the litter and ran to her. She turned, eying him narrowly.

"Aren't you missing out on the festivities?"

"Sonja—It's a long walk."

"I like to walk."

"Get in the palanquin. I'll take you to your apartment."

"The walk'll do me good."

"You'll get your throat slit, this time of night! Come on, Sonja."

"You know I can take care of myself." She looked at him deliberately, scuffling her boots on the stone. There was anger in her eyes.

"Oh, come on," Sendes persisted. "Nalor laughed it off. He was glad you defied Kus."

"Like hell."

"Look, forget about it. There's half a bottle of wine in the litter. Just let me take you back to your place."

Sonja dropped her head, then threw it back with a flourish of her hair and laughed a strange, dark laugh. "Erlik and Tarim!" she said. "All right, all right."

They walked back to the palanquin and got in. The bearers lifted them up, and for the first few minutes of the ride Sonja and Sendes both were silent.

Then, lifting the wine bottle, Sendes asked: "Care for some?"

Sonja shook her head.

"Better dampen that temper," Sendes urged her. "You can't keep up this anger forever."

"You people are fools, do you know that? Damned fools."

"What?"

"Don't you realize what Kus is?" Sonja demanded, turning to him. "Don't you sense it?"

Sendes was taken by surprise. "I'm afraid I don't. I thought he was a trickster."

"A trickster! You people must be blind from years of living in riches and luxury. That man is foul. He's a sorcerer. Those weren't simple tricks. I felt ice in my gut when I saw his eyes."

"You know about sorcerers, do you?" Sendes asked, not serious.

Sonja eyed him belligerently, then borrowed the wine bottle and took a long swallow.

"That's the spirit," Sendes encouraged her. "It's all been forgotten by now. Actually, Nalor surprised me. I thought he'd send me packing, but he didn't. You just took everyone by surprise, that's all."

Sonja handed the bottle back.

"You're full of surprises, I'll bet," Sendes continued. "Aren't you?"

Sonja recognized the tone in his voice.

The Corinthian set the bottle aside, yawned lightly, began whistling a simple tune. And in a moment Sonja felt the brushing whisper of his fingers on her thigh.

"Don't, Sendes," she said evenly.

He did not stop; his fingers continued, his palm pressing upon the fullness of her leg.

"Don't, Sendes, I mean it."

"But you surely—"

She faced him squarely. "Just don't."

Sendes was so surprised that for a moment he still did not remove his hand. Sonja returned it to him, picking it up and dropping it in his lap.

"Sonja . . .?"

"I believe that's my rooming house up ahead."

There was a loud rustle of noise in the litter as Sendes squirmed on his cushions, grumbling. Sonja smiled, not happily.

"Just leave the subject alone," Sonja told him in a quiet voice.

"There's a saying," Sendes remarked brusquely. "Don't you know that a woman who won't is a woman who can't?"

"Funny," she sneered, coldness creeping into her voice, "we have a saying in Hyrkania, too. Don't you know that a man who can't hold his wine can't hold onto his woman?"

Sendes leaned out the window. "Stop here!" he yelled to his bearers.

The palanquin shuddered to a standstill. Sonja opened her curtains and stepped out, closed them again and spoke to Sendes politely. "The party was a good idea," she told him. "I've just got too much of a temper."

"You've got too much of a lot of things. Good night."

He called to his bearers to take him back to Lord Nalor's. Sonja watched the palanquin lurch off down the cobbled street, the slaves panting and sweating as they trotted. Then she turned down the alley, opened the door and climbed the dark stairs to her room.

"Mitra!" she muttered, shaking her head. "Men. . . ."

Her dreams that night were peopled with staring,

laughing faces—rich people, dressed in garments of blood-red and flesh-white, crowded into a room lit by wavering oil lamps. Sonja, in her dream, faced a tall lean wizard who laughed at her, condemned her with his cold eyes and dared her to strike him with her sword. Try as she might, she could not lift the weapon; it grew too heavy in her hand and dropped with a thud. *Strike! strike!* cried the evil magician in her dream, tearing open his robe, baring his breast to her blade. His heart was upon his chest, a purplish-black muscle bulging and pumping thickly, a knot that glistened and throbbed in the oil light. *Strike! strike!* But Sonja could not lift her sword, and the faces—greasy, sweating, grinning with pointed teeth—crowded in close to her and laughed and cackled with malicious glee.

She awoke suddenly—but not because of the dream. Limbs heavy, as if she had been drugged by her nightmare, Sonja sat up in her bed and listened. The noise continued. At her window—

"Hotath's talons . . . !"

She reached across her pillow, drew her sword from the floor, and watched the casement.

Again, the clacking—like pebbles thrown upon the thick glass, or as though an animal's teeth were rattling on it, trying to bite through.

Sonja stood up, sword out. She saw, now, what was at her window. A shadow—a small, lumpy form scraping at the glass. With the silence of a cat she crossed the room, sword up, its blade dully gleaming in the refracted night-light coming in faintly from outside. Naked, she felt the coolness of the room; gooseflesh grew on her arms and legs.

In one motion she unlatched the window and pulled it open. She heard a sharp cry, saw two hands outside trying frantically to find a grip on the stone ledge.

"Damn you, what—?"

"*Sonja!*"

A boy's voice—and she recognized it.

The fingers were slipping.

"Mitra!" She dropped her sword, reached out the window and grabbed the white hands. "Chost! What in the name of—?"

"Just help me in, damn it!"

She dragged him in over the ledge. He was breathless. Catching his balance as he fell to the floor, he leaned back against the sill and raised a weak hand to his face.

"Gods!" Chost gasped. "You nearly knocked me off!"

"What the hell do you think you were doing?"

"I could've fallen and been killed!"

"What the hell were you doing on my window ledge, Chost?" Sonja nearly yelled. Then she caught herself. It would do no good to wake up everyone else in the house.

She backed away from Chost, retrieved her sword and laid it down upon the coverlet, then sat beside it on the edge of the bed, watching the boy. Chost was still gaining his breath, but Sonja saw him staring at her, with more than suspicion in his eyes. A dim, gray light filtered into the room and limned her supple long legs, highlighted the ripeness of her full breasts.

"Never see a naked woman before?" she asked Chost.

"Oh, yes."

"Then let's get to the heart of this matter. What were you doing on my window ledge? I just about ran you through—for a second time."

"I came to warn you."

"Warn me?"

"To pay you back. Since you helped me. I was out on the street and I saw some men watching your window."

"What?" Instantly she was up and to the window again, looking out over the sill.

"They're gone now, Sonja."

For an instant she tensed; then, slowly, she went back to the bed and sat down, eying the boy narrowly.

"Chost—how did you know my name?"

"One of the men said it to the others. Red Sonja. He said he went in and asked the landlord which room you were in. I was hiding near them, in the shadows. They didn't see me."

"And how did *you* know which room was mine?"

"I—I followed you here, after you gave me the money. And the next day I watched the house awhile, and saw you looking out this window."

Sonja relaxed a bit, sensing that the boy was telling the truth. "When did the men leave?"

"They left a few minutes ago. That's when I climbed up here. But they were down there for at least an hour."

Sonja considered it. Sendes? "How many men?" she asked.

"Four, I think. Three were wearing armor. One was a tall man in a black robe."

Sonja scowled. Kus, then? Or perhaps Nalor? Probably Kus. "What were they doing?"

"Nothing. Just standing there. I didn't see them do anything. They didn't even talk—except for what I just told you. Are they after you, Sonja?"

Sonja remembered her strange dream and wondered if it had been Kus' doing, somehow. "Did you see what direction they took when they left?"

"North. Up the Street of the Wine-merchants."

North. Towards the government offices and apartments. "Well, Chost, I have a lot to thank you for."

"I—I just wanted to pay you back. Because you helped me."

"Did that money come in handy?"

"Oh, yes. But it's all spent, now."

"All of it? That was a lot of money!"

"Well, there was four of us—and there's a lot more. There's Stiva's sister, and then there's—"

"All right, all right." Sonja watched him for a moment. Chost's eyes wandered around the room, fixed on the table in the middle of the floor. She had some food there: two apples, half a loaf of bread, some cheese and wine. "Are you hungry, Chost?"

"Oh, no, no, no! I just stole some food from the back of a bakery shop."

"Ah. I see. Because I've got some food over there and—you can help yourself, if you want to."

"Well. . . ." He looked at the food, at Sonja, back at the food. "Maybe—an apple. I haven't had an apple in a while."

"Well, go ahead, by all means. Help yourself to an apple."

"And maybe a little bit of cheese. . . ."

Sonja dressed and sat on the bed, amused, and watched as Chost proceeded to eat everything she had set out on the table.

"Bakery shop, huh?"

"Well, maybe that was earlier this morning. Or last night."

"What're you going to do now, Chost?"

He burped slightly. "Oh, I don't know. Get back to my friends, I guess."

"If you're tired, you're welcome to sleep here."

His eyes lit up. "With you?"

"On the floor, Chost. There's another blanket in the closet."

"Oh." He sounded disappointed. "That's too bad."

"Too bad, huh?"

"You're a nice-looking lady."

Sonja smiled wryly. "Thanks, but I've been through that once tonight already. Why don't you just get some sleep? Just don't let the landlord find you. I'll be back in a little while." She headed for the stairs.

"Where are you going? Wait!"

"I'll be back after a while."

"I'm going with you!

"Chost, just get some sleep."

"No-ohh-no! You can't go out there by yourself."

"I promise you, I can take care of myself."

"But those men might still be out there."

"I told you I can take care of myself. I want to find out who they are."

"But I saw them," Chost protested. "I can tell you exactly where they went. I'll know them when I see them."

It was logical. And Chost knew the streets of Shadizar better than Sonja did. "All right, Chost. Come on along. . . ."

Quietly, they went down the stairs, three floors of them, and out the back door into the alley. Sonja smelled something peculiar. Chost, not sensing anything, commented: "The tall one was standing right here."

"Oh, really?"

"Yes. Then they took off in this direction. They had a carriage waiting further up the way."

"Uh-huh." Sonja started walking, north—for what, exactly, she wasn't sure. Certainly she did not expect to find Kus and three of Count Nalor's guards waiting for her in a carriage several blocks farther up.

But she knew she couldn't sleep. She had been afraid

that her sudden, rash action at the feast would bring some kind of retaliation—just what, she wasn't sure. Nalor might not have given a damn, himself, but Kus was another matter. There was a hard, vindictive evil about him. He had people believing that he was no more than some sort of trickster, and Sonja's accusation of him in public would doubtless prove difficult for Kus to accept. No matter that Sonja was a barbarian, a stranger and a woman in man's armor. She had done enough, just by declaring Kus a sorcerer; even if she were believed a mad woman, suspicions would still be gossiped about, the damage would still be done. Kus couldn't allow her to continue going about and saying such things—not if he wanted to keep his true nature a secret.

What form of retaliation the sorcerer might attempt, Sonja could only speculate; and trying to outguess a sorcerer was akin to guessing what the weather might be like a hundred days from now. But if Kus were like other sorcerers she had encountered, he would retaliate. Somehow.

Mitra knew, it wasn't in her nature to back down from a fight! Yet, she did not relish inviting trouble in Shadizar. All she had wished was to find employment somewhere, or idle away a few pleasant days before saddling up and heading on, if pickings proved slim. And now, here she was, run afoul of a powerful politician and the sorcerer he kept on a leash. Or, was it the other way around?

Sonja shook her head, sensing a maze of confusion ahead of her; like a vague dream, some of the events of the past day or two returned to her mind: Count Endithor's execution, Sendes and Areel in the tavern, Nalor, and now Kus—a magician, or even worse, a sorcerer.

Sonja wondered ruefully, not for the first time, if part of her destiny included her being trouble-prone.

"Sonja!" Chost called out, in a tight whisper.

They had walked several blocks, with Sonja lost in her reveries and not paying full attention to the street, save for peripheral, unconscious awareness of night-haunters crossing the avenue they were following north, noises from distant taverns, gongs proclaiming the hour from some of the temples. Now, at Chost's cry—subdued with alarm—she was instantly aware, gloved hand to sword-pommel, half-crouched and poised to move, chin forward, eyes alert.

"Down there, Sonja! Look!"

They were not far from the nobles' apartments, in fact. The streets were fairly well lighted, and Sonja saw in the glow of wall-set torches, far down at the end of an alley, a young woman hurrying away from them.

Sonja ran to the alley-entrance, gripped the corner of the building with one hand, watched the woman. "Chost, she's no danger to us. She's only a servant—"

"Someone's following her!" he hissed.

"All right, stay back. Keep quiet."

As the last word left her lips, she saw what Chost had seen—a shadow, large and bulky, scuttling behind the woman. It made no sound, although the clatter of the woman's clogs sounded rapid and loud on the pavement. Sonja tensed. She would have cried out to warn the woman—

An instant's indecisiveness—indecisiveness born from Sonja's doubt, now, that there actually was a pursuer. Because she had seen what Chost had seen, and not seen: a scuttling shadow that leapt in the pools of darkness in the alley—and then disappeared.

"It's there!" Chost whispered, as if reading the doubts in Sonja's mind.

"Chost, I—"

Then it reappeared—and so swiftly did the attack come that even if Sonja had wanted to cry out an alarm to the woman, it would never have done any good.

The hurrying woman was passing beneath a torch, and as she moved from under the light the shadow leapt upon her. She screamed—but as the shadow wrapped about her, the scream dwindled and issued only as a muffled gurgle. Immediately the shadow, much larger than she, engulfed her like a living, black fog. Two brilliant, yellow-glowing diamonds showed for a moment. The woman gargled again, was suddenly thrown or tilted back—and then hidden entirely by darkness.

Sonja was dashing forward, pulling free her sword. It scraped the side of the brick building as it cleared the sheath, and sparks shot. The shadow moved, alerted.

"Get away from her, damn you!" Sonja yelled. "Stand back, damn it!"

She was already half-way down the alley, her bootsteps echoing sharply in the night—but before she was even fairly close to the woman and her attacker, the shadow dropped back. The woman fell into view, pale and limp, as the shadow let go of her; she dropped to the ground, and her head cracked sharply on the stone flags.

Sonja swung her sword and charged. "Eat steel, damn you!" she howled.

But the shadow leapt back—a tall, black shadow without definite form save for two ghostly yellow lamps for eyes. In a moment of unreality it spread out its black, wavering substance, seemed to dissolve into a cloud of gas or smoke—and then vanished.

Utterly, leaving no trace.

"Gods!" Chost yelled, from far behind Sonja.

Never slackening her speed, Sonja leapt over the prone body of the woman and hacked the air where the shadow had been. If it had turned invisible, steel might yet wound it—But her blade passed through only empty air, and no resistance rewarded her furious strokes.

"Erlik's Hells!" she cursed. Quickly she ran on to the end of the alley, looked up and down both directions of the street. Only the night's stillness met her.

No shadow.

Furious, tingling with anger, she turned back towards the woman.

Chost was already kneeling beside her, and Sonja now saw, in the light of the torch on the wall, that the woman was dressed in cheap garments and wooden clogs. Her face was white—pale, deathly white—and her white face, framed by dark auburn hair, was resting lifelessly in a widening pool of blood.

Damn! Sonja thought. *He's broken her neck!*

But Chost, bent close to the woman, feeling her flowing blood staining his fingers, suddenly looked up at Sonja with wide, fearful eyes.

"Sonja. . . ."

"She's dead, Chost."

"Look, Sonja. . . ." in a trembling voice.

Sonja hunched down, peered closer. Chost had wiped away at the woman's throat; and now that the blood was rilling less lavishly from her wound, it showed clearly upon the flesh. Not a broken neck, nor even a slash mark—at least, not a mark made by knife or any other kind of blade. Just two wounds—ragged punctures, torn or gouged into the throat with great force, and other teeth marks around.

"Erlik!" Sonja whispered, in a cold breath.

Chost was almost crying in his fear. "This is not the

first one like this!" he confided to Sonja in an agitated, small voice. "There have been others during the past few months—the same kinds of deaths. Few talk about them, but we know—my friends and I; people are dying like this, all the same." And then, his voice faint, he said the word that Sonja was already thinking, the only possible word, the only explanation for what lay in this alley between them: *"Ilorku!"*

Ilorku—originally a Stygian word, Sonja knew, but now belonging to the vocabularies of every race and every nation in the world. Ilorku.

Vampire.

And then, making an immediate connection, Sonja wondered what kind of hold Kus had upon Nalor, and what kind of hellish phantoms the sorcerer was releasing upon Shadizar. . . .

Chapter 4.

In reading through her father's diaries, Areel had discovered not only what magic her father had learned, but where he had learned it—and from whom.

There was, apparently, an old witch named Osumu living in the tenement district of Shadizar. Endithor described her in detail, gave her location, wrote down all that she had told him, and listed all her articles, both those which she had given him and those which she still possessed—articles by which she plied her craft. Following his typically bureaucratic habit, Endithor had made note of all of it in his spidery hand.

So it was to a witch named Osumu—the very word seemed to connote Zamoran words for strangeness and darkness—that Areel knew she must turn to effect her revenge. Already she felt that she knew enough to accomplish small things. Sorcery—magic—was simply a discipline; one wished to accomplish certain things, so one found or created the tools by which to accomplish those things. It was as simple as that. The only thing was that sorcery involved using stranger tools than those used in more mundane pursuits, and there was always a risk. For some of those tools involved communication with beings that were less—or more—than human.

Areel pondered upon her plan, and then suppressed a yawn. She had been up half the night, studying her father's diaries; when she had finally retired, at three chimes, she had only tossed and turned and waited futilely for slumber. So she had arisen again at five chimes. And now, as the temple gongs were announcing the twelfth hour after darkness and the beginning of the new day, she stretched, set aside the volumes and scrolls and journals, and got up from her bed.

There was a small knock on the outer door. Areel pulled aside the drapes that formed a purdah around her bed, went to the door and opened it. "Come in, Lera."

"I have prepared your bath, mistress."

"All right."

While Lera went around the room, dousing oil lamps, Areel pulled back her dark hair and pinned it, then removed her sleeping robe, drew on her sandals and draped a loose, light chiton about her. She left her room and went down the hall to the bath. It was remarkable, she reflected, the things wealth and power could bring one; a private bathing chamber, for example.

Even the warm soapy waters could not entirely relax Areel's tension, but after rising from the bath, she softened a bit beneath her masseur's ministrations. By the time Lera came in to rub her down with oils and help her with her hair, Endithor's daughter was feeling awake and refreshed and in charge of herself.

Her breakfast was waiting for her in her room, but Areel did not eat much of it. Lera, coming in presently to remove the trays, remarked upon it.

"I'm just not hungry," Areel told her. "Do I have to explain myself to my girl-servants?"

"No, mistress, no. I'm sorry." Lera fluttered around the trays, putting dishes back on them. Accidentally she knocked over a goblet of wine; the silver clanged on the floor and the wine spilled out upon one of the carpets.

"What's the matter with you?" Areel complained angrily. "You're as nervous as a cat!"

"I'm sorry, mistress! I'm sorry! Please. . . ."

"Lera, what's gotten into you?"

The girl, retrieving the goblet, almost dropped it again as she replaced it on the tray. "I'm—I'm just very upset, mistress. I think it's because there was another murder last night."

"Another murder?"

"You know. . . ."

"Oh. Oh." Areel showed her concern for a moment.

"It just frightens me so much, Mistress Areel. I'm afraid of—of the—"

"You're safe enough, as long as you're here. You don't go out walking the streets at night, do you?"

"No, mistress!"

"Well, then, you're safe enough. Now call Tirs and have him take out this carpet. And call Siloum to prepare one of the palanquins. I'm going out this morning."

"Yes, Mistress Areel." Lera hurried out of the room, juggling the tray in her hands.

When she was gone, Areel, murmuring something about silly slave-wenches, looked out the window at the city of Shadizar—looked to the southern side of the city, where the tenements were.

Osumu's lodgings were in a particularly squalid section of the south side. Areel had her bearers—four of them, the only slaves other than Tirs who had not abandoned her—wait just outside the rundown apartment house. The well-dressed servants and the richly decorated litter caused something of a commotion on the street; poor people on this side of town, though accustomed to seeing gentry pass through, were not often able to inspect the finer things of life at close hand. But none came too close. And the city patrols, making their rounds, kept an obvious eye on the litter and the slaves, knowing it could only serve their best interests to stay on the right side of whoever owned such impressive goods.

Areel walked down a side-alley, opened a door that led directly to a worn staircase. Down the hall, to the right of the stairs, she could hear caterwauling and confusion. The building apparently served only as a dwelling; there was no tavern on the ground floor.

On the second floor landing, being careful not to spoil her fine sandals by stepping into any of the piles of rubbish or refuse, Areel looked for the door with the sign of the hawk on it. Half-way down the hall, and past a rancid-smelling old oil pot, she found it, and rapped loudly. There was no answer; she rapped again, and then again. Could the old woman be absent? Hard of hearing?

At last, muffled, from within: "Who is it?" in a voice like that of an old bird.

"I wish to speak with you, Osumu. I know who you are."

"Who is it? Tell me!"

"I am Endithor's daughter. Let me speak with you!"

Slowly the door opened a crack; part of a gray, wrinkled face appeared shoulder-high before Areel, and a bright eye, discolored yellow with a black pupil, roved up and down.

"Endithor's daughter?" rasped the crow-like voice.

"Areel. Did he ever mention me?"

"No. I heard he might have had a daughter."

Areel showed the eye of her right hand; on the index finger was a ring, its stone carved in the seal of Endithor's house. "Proof enough?"

The eye blinked a few times, looked up and down again. "No. How do I know you are really Endithor's daughter, hey?"

"Old witch, who else would have anything to do with you, after what has happened?"

The door closed again, and there was a rasping and a clacking sound behind it, as though a chain were being drawn through iron eyes. Then it opened, and the old woman stood back. Areel entered cautiously, looking in every direction.

"Close the door, please, daughter of Count Endithor."

Areel turned softly. She was carrying a heavy leather bag on her left arm; now she shifted it to the crook of her elbow for comfort, then closed the door, and saw that there was indeed an arrangement for locking it with a chain.

"What do you want here?" old Osumu asked. There was something like apprehension in her wavering, croaking tones.

Areel faced her. "I am not here to harm you, be assured. I am investigating my father's death—or, rather, the trumped-up charges that led to his arrest. I suspect that Lord Nalor is behind it. Is he?"

The old woman did not reply, merely fixed Areel with her stark gaze.

"May I sit?"

Osumu shrugged. She motioned Areel to cross the room, then sat herself upon a woven reed mat in one corner, behind a low table. Areel studied the old woman, and the room, as she settled herself on another mat. Osumu was thin as a wren, brown and gray and wrinkled. Her clothing was a motley of old fabrics and animal skins, and she was decorated as well with trinkets and gems and bits of carved bone.

The room mirrored her. Small, stinking with old incenses and perfumes and refuse, it was cluttered everywhere with wooden boxes, with clay pots full of pungent-smelling spices and oils, with old scrolls and wood-bound books, with bronze and iron incense braziers, skulls, carved stone-work, glass objects, rugs and tapestries woven with strange designs—all the occult ornaments one might have expected to find in a witch's den.

Areel, now sitting cross-legged opposite her hostess beside the low table, set to one side the leather bag she had brought along.

"Now," she began, countering the suspicious glare in Osumu's eyes with her own determined gaze, "I want the facts behind my father's death. I know he came to you for certain items and certain knowledge regarding the use of sorcery. Did Lord Nalor send him to you?"

"No." The quickness of old Osumu's answer surprised Areel.

"You are not lying to me?"

"Count Endithor came to me of his own volition. He mentioned Lord Nalor; but Nalor never spoke to me. Nalor does not know that I exist; he would not care if he knew. But I imagined your father came to me because of what lives in Nalor's house."

"What do you mean—'what' lives in Nalor's house?"

"Kus." She spoke it with a serpent's breath, slithering the word at the end with a susurrus.

"Kus?"

"And is that not why you are here?" Osumu

smiled—if the skewing of her wrinkled lips could be considered a smile.

"I know that Nalor caused my father to be arrested and executed. I know that Nalor did this to protect himself."

"To protect himself, maybe. To hide the secret of Kus, certainly. He fears Kus."

"Why?"

"Because Kus is evil. Did your father never say anything of him?"

"Only a few things."

Osumu shrugged. "Only the things he felt you needed to know. Kus is evil. Far more evil than Nalor, who is only human."

"Kus is a sorcerer?"

Osumu barked a whining laugh, showing her toothless mouth. "Call him a sorcerer, if you will. Names do not mean that much to the evil ones. Humans feel they know something if they give it a name. But the evil are simply the evil."

Areel pondered that for a moment. Then she changed the subject. "I know that you taught my father magic."

"I taught him how to do certain things, yes."

"And you sold him, or gave him, certain implements by which to work sorcery."

"I may have done so."

"Despite this—or because of it—my father was found out. Nalor ordered my father to use sorcery against Kus, but he had no intention of allowing my father to succeed. It was all a ruse. And you tell me that Nalor does not know you?"

"Your father could have gone to many, many places in Shadizar the Wicked to find out how to work magic. Do you think Nalor cares where he went?"

"I want you to tell me that."

"Young woman—daughter of Endithor—I gave your father the magic means by which to do what he wished to do. This is true. But there are a hundred witches in this city who might have done the same, and a hundred men claiming to be sorcerers who might also have done it. There are outlander shamans and renegade priests and fortune-tellers who might have done it as well."

"But most of these are frauds. The magic you gave him—it would have worked?"

"Pfah!" Osumu made a throaty sound. "The magic is there for anyone. The incenses and the candles, the cries and the chants—" The old woman shrugged. "Without belief, these things are useless, but if the belief and the will are there, the magic works. The demons and the spirits, they are always waiting. They are in dreams and in wine. If you want the aid of demons, call on them. Light your candles, burn your smoke—this makes it easier. But the demons will come, anyway. The demons are in your heart, and in mine. The incense does not cause the demons to come; we use the incense, and we invite the demons. If you want to work magic, begin to practice it. Nothing else is very important. The demons and spirits are there, and they will come if you invoke them. Do you pray to the gods?"

"Sometimes."

"Do the gods answer you? Do they come to you?"

"I don't know. Sometimes . . . maybe. They are mysterious."

"But the demons are not so mysterious. They come more quickly. The gods are distant; the demons are close. The demons come quickly for the quick feast; they hunger, always. Always. The gods do not hunger like the demons hunger."

Areel pondered this. Could it be accomplished so easily? "But you taught my father magic. You gave him the things to work it. I want you to teach me, as well."

Osumu watched her.

Now Areel bent to her leather bag and began to produce an assortment of items. "You gave these things to my father—or, he bought them from you. Is that not true?"

"It may be true."

Areel set the items on the table: two scrolls, some candles, a talisman, a stone phial of some oil or other liquid.

"You did," Areel insisted.

Osumu again displayed what seemed to be her smile and leaned forward, reaching for a pitcher and two bronze cups that sat on the table. "Let us sip wine while we talk."

Areel did not trust her; she did not want to drink Osumu's wine. "Did my father pay you well for these things?"

"Aye. He paid me well. Drink your wine."

"I have money—all my father's money. I can pay you as well as he did, or better."

Osumu cackled. "Money? What need have I for money? Your father did not pay me in money."

Areel was taken aback. "In what, then?"

"Drink your wine, young woman."

"Slaves? Did you demand slaves of him? Or things for your sorcery which you did not yet possess?"

Osumu said nothing.

"Did you buy his soul, old woman?"

"I demanded—him," she muttered. "Please—drink." Then she suddenly began cackling. "The payment I demanded from your father was that he make love to me! Does that shock you? Ah-ha-ha! Yes, yes!

Do you not have desires, young woman? Do you think those desires die when your body grows old?"

Thinking of her father, Areel was, indeed, momentarily shocked. But she was also good at keeping her emotions to herself. Answering Osumu's laughter with only a contemptuous smile, Areel at last decided that she would take no more from this revolting old woman. She reached into her bag for one last object.

"Drink your wine, Endithor's daughter."

"In a moment, when I have concluded my business. Do you know this?" She held out the dagger Endithor had used in his ritual.

"It is possible."

"Did you sell my father this magical dagger, as well?"

Osumu's eyes narrowed. "I may have. What is your purpose in—?"

"I want you to look at it, Osumu." Areel leaned forward, slowly. The gold work upon the dagger glinted in the dull light of the lamps; the tip of the blade pointed directly toward the old woman. Osumu, suddenly fearful, began to shrink away.

"Look, now," Areel indicated, "at the imprint on the blade, near the haft—"

And then she moved. The dagger-point, only a hand-length from Osumu's face, jumped forward; books and goblets clattered to the floor.

Osumu jerked back, more quickly than Areel would have believed possible. Still, the blade-tip had caught the old witch on her cheek; a thin line of blood stood out darkly on the gray, wrinkled flesh.

"Young whore!" Osumu rasped. "Is this why you—?" Then, abruptly, the words strangled in her throat and she said no more.

Areel sat back, wiped the blade of her dagger on the reed mat. Osumu, still crouched, fell backwards awkwardly, bumping into the wall, sliding into a grotesque cross-legged position. Her eyes burned with wrath upon Areel. Her throat rattled—but she could not speak. Her hands shivered, her fingers tightened up into bony claws—otherwise, she could not move them.

"Some juice from the *ding* plant, old witch," Areel said casually. "It will kill you, eventually. For now, it is enough that you are wholly paralyzed." Quickly replacing the items she had brought in her leather bag, Areel then reached for her wine goblet, which had not spilled. As she brought the cup to lips, her eyes settled on Osumu's.

"No-o," Areel decided. "Perhaps I am not so thirsty, after all. What, Osumu? Would you have me drink? Would you, old witch? Am I right in suspecting some poison, perhaps, in this cup?"

Osumu's eyes dimmed; still, she stared at Areel.

"I believe, indeed, that I do suspect some poison, Osumu. Perhaps I had better not drink it myself. Perhaps I should have someone test it for me, eh?" Areel rose. Carrying the cup, she moved around the low table and bent over the crone, whose eyes, because she could not tilt her head, rolled up in anguish. "Test it, witch!"

She put the lip of the cup to Osumu's partially-open mouth and tilted it; much wine spilled down the witch's front, but some seemed to seep between her teeth.

For a moment Areel watched, deliberating. "Not taking effect very quickly, is it, Osumu? And that *ding* poison will take till nightfall to kill you. Painful, yes—and it is well that you should suffer, because of your part in what happened to my father. But you'll still be alive when I leave, and I can't risk that. What if I poured some of this poisoned wine into your eyes?"

Osumu let out a hoarse breath—her faint, impotent attempt at a scream.

83

"Yes, yes. Poison in the eyes should get into the blood very quickly, I would think. Just seep all the way into your brain, I would guess. Into your brain—itch at your bones. Don't you think so, Osumu?"

Another hoarse gasp, frightful. . . .

Areel tilted the cup above Osumu's forehead. Trickles of wine drained from it into both of Osumu's eyes. The crone faintly kicked with one foot; otherwise, there was no real outward show of her anguish.

Having now vented her spite, Areel did not wait for Osumu to die but turned away from her in disgust. Very quickly she moved around the room and began stuffing her large leather bag with items she thought might be of use to her in her magic. Much, she guessed, was worthless: statues, ornaments, and so on. Other things—herbs, incenses, candles, knives—she could readily acquire herself and consecrate for use in sorcerous ritual. She already knew enough, from what she had read in her father's diaries and books, to know which amulets, grimoires and other articles to take: things already imbued with dark power, things already ancient and charged with taints of demonism.

All such things that she could find Areel stuffed into her bag. Then, without a backward glance at the dying witch, she went out the door, closed it carefully behind her, and stole down the hallway.

But she paused at the bottom of the stairs, behind the wall that hid her from the hallway on the ground floor. Someone—the landlord, most likely—was yelling in wrath at a young man and woman, screaming for them to get their trash together and leave his house forever. Areel peeked around the corner. The young pair seemed to be moving out from the room directly below Osumu's.

When the couple had gone and the landlord had

stomped off, Areel shouldered her pack, went out the alley door and returned to her palanquin. She did not hurry or otherwise act suspiciously. By this time there were no longer any curious loiterers surrounding her conveyance or slaves, and no city guards within view.

It was noon, and the heat of the sun was making it uncomfortable in these narrow, odorous lanes. Areel ordered her men to bear her home; once there, she promised herself, she would have a meal, then study her books and magical objects all afternoon, so that tonight she would be ready to begin her revenge against Nalor.

The Dragon Seed Tavern that night roared with bravado and camaraderie and gusto. Sendes, too, roared with the best of them; for he was there, as he was every night of the week, challenging all comers to his latest fascination, the throwing of knives. He stood in the corner at the far wall, lifting his cup of beer now and then, spilling foam as he laughed at rude jests, and not getting quite serious even as he stepped to the line, his money on the line as well, and lifted knife to aim for the bull's eye.

It was in the mid-evening, while the wine and beer were flowing well and tempers had not yet overturned, that Areel entered the Dragon Seed. Rough fellows stayed out of her way as she crossed the floor, not wanting to invite trouble from her end of town. Sendes had just won another cup of beer, and was laughingly poking fun at his defeated competitor, when his eyes fell upon his old flame. His smile slackened; he did not raise his cup to his lips; he looked left and right, looked at Areel again, and stood up from his seat.

Areel floated toward him, more astonishingly beautiful in the crude lamplight of the tavern than she might have been in the softer glow of her chambers' tapers and shaded oil lights—or so it seemed to Sendes in that moment.

"You on for the next throw, Sen?" asked one of his companions.

"No, no. Go on without me. . . ." He moved his cup to another table, gestured for Areel to meet him there. She skirted the packed corner of the barroom, nodded graciously to Sendes as he pulled out a chair for her. She sat, held her head high and rested her chin on slender fingers.

Sendes studied her defensively. "What is it tonight, Areel?"

Many other eyes than Sendes' were upon her, however. Areel knew it; she looked around the room, playing innocent, as if deciding upon which rude patron she might choose as tonight's lover. "I only wish to speak with you, Sendes."

"Not more questions about Nalor?" He spoke in a low tone.

"No. No more about Nalor."

"Because I'm in enough trouble with him already, if you must know. I've got to—"

"No more about Nalor," Areel reassured him, and softly lay her hand on his own.

"—got to watch it for a while. Made a real mistake the other night. . . ."

"Shhh, Sendes. I only want to ask one small favor of you."

"—the other night. . . ." Her hand on the back of his felt to Sendes very warm. Extremely warm. And now, as he looked into Areel's eyes, Sendes seemed to notice how strange they were. They seemed to pulse.

"No, we won't talk about Nalor," Areel was saying to him. "But I do want to ask one small favor of you. It does have to do with Nalor, I'm afraid. Sendes, I want you to—"

Once, a few months ago, Sendes had seen a regiment captain who owned a small lodestone; and with the lodestone the captain had caused iron fillings to form themselves in strange, cursive patterns upon a sheet of parchment—an interesting display of natural force. Sendes thought of this now, in a comparative but not analytical way, because it seemed to him that his own natural force, his attention, the lights in the room, the focus of his vision, were all following a cursive pattern like those iron filings. His concentration was moving away from him, out from him, and fixing him fast upon Areel's strange eyes and the strange warm feel of her hand. It was almost as if his blood were flowing out of him, in some non-red, non-liquid way.

"—but I want you to speak to Lord Nalor about something for me, Sendes. Will you do that?"

Her voice was soft and warm, like her hand, and deep and resonant, like her eyes. Everything in the world was within Areel's eyes. Sendes could hear her voice, but not in a normal way; her voice pulsed and vibrated and drove into his brain so that it seemed an echo of thoughts he was already thinking.

"I want you to speak with him about my father, Sendes," Areel was saying. "Will you do that, Sendes? For me? And I want you to be forceful. I don't want you to let Nalor talk you out of anything. I think it would be best if you pulled out your sword, just to let him know that you are serious and masterful. Do you understand, Sendes, my love?"

Of course he understood. It only made sense; perfect sense. It was only natural that he should do this, not only for himself and Areel but for all of Shadizar. Around him, dying out now, as the sound of the surf dies out as one heads inland, were the brawling noises of the tavern.

"Do you understand, Sendes, my love?"

"Yes, of course I understand . . . Areel."

"Shall you do it now?"

"Yes, of course."

"Come, I'll take you in my palanquin. All right?"

"Yes. Of course. . . ."

They rose up, Areel still holding her hand to Sendes'. That was important, Sendes felt; he feared that if Areel removed her hand, he would suffocate or collapse, fall dead without her support.

They moved through the tavern, Areel leading, Sendes following like a drunken man being dragged home by a disappointed little sister. Behind them, as they left, came the call of one of Sendes' companions:

"Sendes! Where're you going? We're starting a new game!"

"Oh, let him go," said another man.

"Sendes! One last game!"

"Oh, Chor, let him go. A pretty fanny'll do it every time."

A third man laughed, correcting him: "A *rich* pretty fanny, my friend. Aye, aye!—a *rich* pretty fanny. . . ."

Outside, the cool evening air did not affect Sendes, did not awaken his mind or revitalize him. Dependent upon Areel's touch, he hastened in order to hold onto her as she led him to her palanquin.

To the ride north up the main boulevard he paid no attention. He heard only his own thoughts as translated or interpreted by Areel. Yes, yes, have a talk with Nalor, take out my sword, yes. I'm a good swordsman, one stroke will do it, and have a talk with Nalor. Endithor was murdered, Nalor behind it, make that clear, the city won't stand for it, and have a little talk with Nalor. . . .

When the litter stopped, Areel directed Sendes' attention out the window. He recognized the front of Lord Nalor's apartment.

"I'm going to let go of you now, Sendes."

"No, no, no. . . ."

"You'll be all right. You'll be fine. You'll be strong enough to find Nalor and talk with him and finish the talk. Do you understand?"

"Yes. . . ."

"Good. Go on, now. Yes, yes, go on."

When she lifted her hand from his, Sendes felt a jolt throughout his entire body. He felt suddenly very weak and ill; but that sensation passed in a moment, and as he climbed down from the litter he took in several deep breaths, hoisted one hand to his sword-pommel, faced the walk-way leading to the front portico of Lord Nalor's house.

"Go on, now, Sendes," Areel's voice told him. "Go on, now. . . ."

He walked, not really feeling his boots striking on the hard stone. As he made his way up the walk, he did not hear Areel's slaves lift up her litter and move back down the boulevard without him.

Up the walk—up the stairs. . . .

At the entrance were two servants who recognized him. They nodded to him and opened the portals, bidding him good evening—but Sendes did not return the greeting.

Down the foyer entrance-way he strode. It was the middle of the evening, so Nalor would most likely be in his study at the end of the first hall. . . . Sendes turned down the hall, passed a slave-girl carrying an empty tray. So—she must have just served Nalor. Kus might or might not be with Nalor; that didn't matter. Kus was no part of this. The argument was between Nalor and Sendes.

He rapped upon the door five times with the knocker, in the sequence that would let his employer know that it was a member of the guard awaiting entrance.

"Come in," sounded Nalor's voice.

Sendes lifted the latch on the heavy door, opened it, stepped in and pushed the portal closed behind him.

"Ah, Sendes. Good evening. You look a little drunk, young man. At the tavern again, I take it? What's on your mind?"

Nalor was alone. The study was not large; the nobleman was sitting at his desk, a pitcher of wine to hand, a parchment unrolled before him and his pens in the open ink well. Sendes approached, hand tightening on his sword-pommel.

"Sendes? What ails you, fellow?" Nalor stood up, his hands on the top of the desk.

Sendes felt a shudder rip through him, felt his senses coming back. A fog seemed gradually to be lifting—a fog that weakened him and strengthened him intermittently. For one moment he felt like collapsing to the floor; the next, Areel's voice sounded like a gong in his brain. He saw Nalor as through a sheet of red flame, and anger and terror churned within him.

"Sendes? Sendes!"

His hand tightened more firmly on his sword. One moment aware of the feeling of carved metal, he lost the sensation in the next, did not understand that he had pulled his longsword from its sheath.

"Sendes! What in the names of the gods—?"

Nalor was backing away—trying, now, to run around his desk, to reach the sword-rack on the floor by the oil brazier.

Sendes screamed—from fear and anger. Sword out, he ran forward. Nalor, half a room away from the sword-rack, slipped and fell.

"Sendes!"

"For . . . *Endithor!"* he screamed, and swung down his sword furiously.

Nalor rolled; Sendes' blade struck the stone tiles with a clang. A shiver of tension ran up the steel and up Sendes' arm.

"Guards! Guards!" Nalor sprang up frantically and ran from the sword-rack, grabbed for the rope by the desk that would alert his household. "Guards!"

As in a half-awake dream, Sendes heard boots on the tiles outside. He should have locked the door. He should run for the window—the tall window, right there, beside the sword-rack. . . . Sendes lifted his sword again, started toward Nalor.

"Guaaaards!"

More bootsteps, together with yells and curses. Nalor, crouched behind his desk, stared in fear at Sendes, stared impotently at the sword-rack.

There was heavy pounding on the door.

"Enter, damn you!" screamed Nalor.

Sendes, sword dragging on the stone, turned and ran for the window.

"Take him! There! Hurry! *Take him!"*

Sonja had just returned to her apartment. It was early yet, but she had spent an exhausting day accomplishing nothing—looking for work, trying to get one particularly belligerent blackguard to pay a swordswoman a share of gold equal to what he paid his male soldiers for the same position on his caravan. To top it off, this evening—wanting only to enjoy a restaurant-meal she'd treated herself to—Sonja had foolishly let herself be goaded into a political argument by some hot-headed student, some yammering rebel who compensated with noise for what he lacked in sense. Enough had been more than enough, and Sonja had been forced to douse the rascal with the last of her ale; that had brought laughs from the other patrons, and on that note—in a bad humor—she had trudged back to her room for an early night's rest.

Now all she wanted was to undress, get to sleep and dream of wide, frosty plains under argent moonlight, far from cities. But luck still would not look in her direction, for no sooner had she put out the oil lamp on her wash table and got under the covers, than there was a tremendous clatter of boots on the outside stairs— and then a frantic pounding on her door.

"Mother of Mitra! If that maniac in the tavern has brought his band of simpletons to my room—!"

She jumped from bed and grabbed up her sword, prepared out of frustration to carve whoever was on the other side of that door. No need to dress; the sight of a naked swordswoman might throw the jackass off just long enough for her to skewer him through the belly. . . .

"Sonja! Sonja, open up!"

She crossed the room, undid the bolt, threw back the door. "In the name of—! Sendes!"

He ran in, threw himself against the side wall, wiping his sweating face and gasping for breath. "Close the door!"

"What in hell are you—?"

"Sonja, close the door!"

Uncertain, she slammed it shut.

"Bolt it!" He still gasped for air.

She did so. "Now, damn it, will you tell me—?"

"They may have seen me come in here," Sendes

rasped. "Quickly, Sonja, I beg of you! Can't you *hide* me somewhere?"

"Hide you?"

"Gods!" he groaned, nearly on the brink of tears, his throat rattling from utter fear. "If they find me, they'll *kill* me, Sonja! Just hide me, if you can!"

"Erlik's throne . . . !" She took a moment to study Sendes; there was no doubt that he felt in grave peril . . . and now, outside, she heard the first commotion of horses and boots on the pavement, and the cry of voices.

"They saw me!" Sendes cried in desperation.

"Quiet!" Swiftly Sonja looked around the room; there were no closets big enough to hide Sendes, and in any event that was too obvious. There was nowhere he might—

"Sendes! Here!" She dragged a chair from the corner across the floor boards, then looked upwards. In the middle of the ceiling the square of a hinged wooden trap door could barely be made out. "It leads to the attic, I think. The landlord was up here this morning, poking around for something. Get on the chair, Sendes!"

He hastily obeyed, while the rising thunder of city troops began to fill the apartment house. Voices cursed and yelled two stories below.

"Push it!" Sonja yelled to him.

With a desperate lurch Sendes shoved the door; it creaked back on rusty hinges.

"Pull yourself up! Hurry, damn you!"

He drew his sword from its scabbard and threw it up before him. A short jump, and he caught both sides with his arms; hurriedly he hauled himself up, drew back from the opening and shut the door.

Sonja could hear the troops on the second floor, just

below. Not wanting to make any betraying noise, she carried the chair back to its corner, carefully fit her sword into a notch on the floor and lay down on her bed.

Within moments the stampede of boots and the clatter of bared steel resounded on the outside landing. Heavy fists pounded on all the doors of all the rooms along the hall. When the blows thundered at Sonja's door, she did not at first answer.

Again, the tumultuous pounding. "Wake up, in there! Open up, or we'll smash down this door!"

She rolled on the bed; the old wood creaked heavily. Sonja feigned a loud yawn. "What the hell is going on out there?"

"Open this door. Landlord! Have you a key?"

"Keep your boots on, keep your boots on!" Sonja cried, getting out of bed, retrieving her sword and crossing the room. She opened the door with a flourish and stood, naked in the dim light, before the small shadowed hall crammed with Zamoran city guards.

All of them were stunned for a moment at the sight of the statuesque, nude Hyrkanian woman with shoulders thrown defiantly back and sword in right hand.

"Now, what in the name of Mitra's mother is going on?"

"We disturbed your sleep, eh?" challenged the foremost guardsman, regaining his wits.

"Kind of looks that way, doesn't it?"

"You carry a sword. Why?"

"I'm a mercenary warrior. Also, I carry it in case rampant fools should come pounding on my door in the night. I like to be prepared."

One hollow voice laughed in the dark hallway; then, it grunted as an anonymous elbow punched into a rib-cage.

"What is your name?" demanded the guardsman.

"Seilissa of Stygia."

The man's eyes narrowed. "Is that your true name?"

"No."

"Tell me your real name."

"You tell me yours, I'll tell you mine. That way, I can register a complaint against you in the morning. Fair?"

"Young woman, you are mocking an officer of the Shadizar City—"

"Guardsman, you woke me out of a sound sleep, and now I'm standing here, getting gooseflesh, while your horny soldiers gawk at me. Now, what the hell do you want? And make it quick!"

Fury purpled the officer's face. He looked past Sonja and surveyed the gray room; then, in a voice full of steely restraint: "We are looking for a soldier of private employ—a criminal, wanted for arrest. He was seen entering this apartment house."

"And you think he's in my room?"

"We think he's somewhere in this house."

"Who wants him arrested? His mother? Or his poor wife?"

"I'm warning you. . . ."

"And I'm warning you! I paid good coppers for this room and I don't like being intruded upon like this! Do you have any legal right to come barging in here?"

The guard snarled a curse. "We don't need any damned legal—!"

"Let me through!" came a voice from the packed crowd, and Sonja recognized it as that of the landlord.

She trembled faintly. If the fat fool thought to have these dogs inspect the attic, she'd have to use her sword. Whatever trouble Sendes had gotten himself into, Sonja—ever instinctively on the side of the underdog against authority—would surely have to side with the foolish young Corinthian.

"Let me through!" came the whiny voice again, and in a moment the fat Zamoran landlord had pushed himself into Sonja's room. He glared at the Hyrkanian. "This is *my* house!" he reminded her angrily. "You paid for the room, but *I* paid for the house, and *I* pay the city taxes on it! Don't you forget that! If I let these troops into this house, it is *my* business, not yours! If I let them into this room, it is *my* prerogative! Do you understand?"

Sonja, reddening with anger, yet held herself in check. Should it come to fighting, she'd see to it that fat-guts was the first to taste steel—but if she lost her temper now, she'd lose her only remaining chance. She had but one last throw of the dice.

"Isn't it possible," she asked, looking again at the officer in charge, "that while you're standing here demanding to get into a naked woman's room, this criminal of yours has already taken advantage of your bumptious stupidity? He's probably crawled out a window and is half-way to Aquilonia by now."

That made sense. With a snarl and a last vindictive look at Sonja, the officer turned to his men. "Quit staring, you bastards—get downstairs and circle the building. Deploy in four directions and begin searching every building and alley in the area! Move! Now!"

The thunder of their exit shook the entire building. As they left, however, Sonja's obese landlord remained standing where he was.

"Put some clothes on," he rasped when the last echo of the troops had faded. "I don't run a whorehouse."

"And I'm not a whore. Anything else?"

"I want you out of here."

"For *what?*" Sonja yelled.

"You're a troublemaker."

"Like hell! You're the one who let those rogues in!"

"Don't you raise your voice to me! I'm landlord here and I can pick and choose my tenants. Understand? I want you out of here!"

"Tonight?" Sonja screamed. "Damn your fat carcass, I paid for my room, and you'll have to call back all those soldiers and then some before I'll let you steal my money!"

The landlord fell back a step at her violent display of temper. Glaring at her, he recovered with: "In the morning, then, Hyrkanian. First thing in the morning!"

"My money's as good as anyone else's!"

"Not to me, it isn't. You could get me in trouble, mouthing off to city guardsmen like that." Then, seeing Sonja's grip tightening on her sword, the landlord blanched and stepped hurriedly back out into the hall. "In the morning!" he howled. "Not one extra moment of daylight for you!"

So saying, he slammed shut the door and left Sonja trembling with rage.

"Damn!" she cried aloud. "Damn, damn, damn him to the Seven Hells!"

Then, from outside her window, she heard more commotion. Curse the gods—! But in an instant she realized that it was boys' laughter—and the ringing of horses' hoofs—and the voices of soldiers crying out threateningly. Sonja went to the window and looked out; in the alley outside she saw a ragged troop of street urchins throwing stones and mud at the city patrol.

"Go on! Go on!" they screamed at the mounted troops. "Guards! Apes! Shiny apes! Get away from here!"

Sonja laughed to hear the popular slang term for the guards. After a few more threats, the soldiers rode off in various directions to pursue their futile search, the nimble urchins following them with taunts and clods of earth.

Still laughing, Sonja leaned over the sill and called out: "Chost! Are you causing more trouble?"

"Hello, Sonja!"

"Go steal some bread!"

Chost and his friends laughed, then ran off.

Sonja turned from the window and crossed the room; reaching up with her sword, she rapped upon the door in the ceiling. "You're safe now, Sendes! Come out!"

As the young soldier lifted the trap and dropped to the floor, Sonja dressed herself in her armor and turned up an oil lamp. Then she poured Sendes what wine remained from the pitcher on her table and handed it to him.

"Drink it. Then, tell me what's happened."

"Gods . . . !" He slurped the wine eagerly.

Sonja turned at the sound of scratching on the window sill; Chost, and three of his pals, were hanging onto the ledge.

"Sonja! Can we come in?"

Sonja nodded. "Come in, Chost." She unlatched the twin panes and swung them inward. "There's a little bread and cheese left. But keep quiet, will you?"

"Aye, Sonja!" They dropped one by one into the room.

Sendes looked at the rag-tag boys, then at the Hyrkanian.

"Friends." Sonja smiled at him. "You're among friends, Sendes. Go on, finish the wine. Then tell me what the hell is going on."

"Gods. . . !" he breathed again, setting down the cup. Sonja motioned toward the chair in the corner, and Sendes sat in it, exhausted and shivering. Chost and his friends crouched on the floor, devouring Sonja's food.

Sonja stretched out on the bed, resting her head on one hand. "Go on, now, Sendes."

He sighed, wiped his face, and then in a humbled, quaking voice began to tell of what had happened this evening—of what he remembered, and of what he feared had happened this evening. . . .

Chapter 5.

An hour before dawn, Lord Count Nalor sat awake in his study, alone with his unread books, his undrunk wine, his unsatisfied wrath. There was still one company of guards out there, somewhere in the city; but the first four companies had returned already, with no Sendes in chains. The traitor had escaped.

Nalor muttered a curse. He had no further plan at the moment, save to send his guards back to the streets, and to send still more after them until they found the young Corinthian dog. On impulse he stood up and reached for the cord to summon one of his men to the study; but just as he would have pulled it, he held back. An inner door had opened, and now Kus strode into the room. Nalor lowered his hand.

The sorcerer did not seem as pale as he had earlier in the night. With lithe control he moved towards Nalor, reached the wide desk and rested his hands softly on the polished wood.

"They did not find the young soldier?" Kus asked, his eyes burning into Nalor's.

"No. The fools."

"You will continue the search?"

"Yes, of course. But if they cannot find him—"

Nalor searched Kus' expression.

"You wish me to aid you, Nalor?"

"Surely you, with your many gifts, can easily track him down and tell me where he is hidden."

Kus shrugged. "It is not so easy as you presume. But, in any event, Sendes is not your enemy. He is only a *subuk*—the smallest piece on the game board, Nalor—and his moves were caused by another. No, he is not your enemy. Last night he was drugged or mesmerized into attacking you."

"Can this be true?"

"Certainly. I can sense some of the power that motivated him, for though it was weak, it lingers here still. Spores in the wind."

"And who *is* my enemy? Not—?"

"Aye. Surely Areel, Endithor's daughter."

"But she does not know sorcery!"

"Neither did Endithor, until you instructed him to gain knowledge of such things. I am sure she hypnotized the young man and sent him to assassinate you."

Nalor shivered with rage. "Then she will be arrested before morning and beheaded before noon!"

"Be careful, Nalor. There are already whisperings behind your back. You must move cautiously."

"I will send an army to her house!"

Kus smiled slightly. "Her magic is hardly so strong, presently. Send an archer to slay her while she sleeps. Make it a secret crime, Nalor; you have too many public crimes on your register already."

Nalor grinned resentfully at Kus. "And your slate is clean? You speak to me of foul crimes, Kus?"

The sorcerer did not bother to reply. He shifted his dark gaze from Nalor to the window at the other side of the room. Blackness was still there, but it would not be long before the first gray of daylight would begin to soften the night's hard edges.

"It will soon be dawn," Kus said softly. "I must be away." He threw out his robe with a flourish, then wrapped it more securely about him.

Nalor stared at him.

"How I distrust the daylight!" Kus went on, looking at Nalor with eyes that seemed to glow with an eerie yellow light. "It is for cowards. The truth cannot long exist in the daylight, Nalor. You and I both know that. People love lies, and tell themselves that truth abides in light; but you and I know that only the night yields the truth. . . ."

With that, he turned and softly left the room. Nalor, still standing within hand's reach of his cord, pulled it. Then he went to his desk, poured himself a small amount from a decanter and, despite the mild headache he had developed, swallowed the wine.

There came a knock on the door.

"Enter!"

In stepped one of Nalor's private household soldiers.

"Who is the best archer in my employ?"

The soldier thought a moment. "Lord Nalor, there is myself, and another man named Suthil."

"Step forward, Hest."

The man did so.

"Any wish you may make that I can fulfill will be granted," said Nalor, "if you carry out my order swiftly and surely. Is that understood?"

"Aye, my lord." Hest was all attention; such opportunities for rapid advance or utter independence were rare. He was prepared to do whatever his master demanded.

"You know the apartment where Lord Endithor resided? Good. His daughter still lives there. Last night, as you know, young Sendes attacked me. Areel, Endithor's daughter, was the cause. She must be killed."

"Aye, my lord."

"Take your bow with you, and the truest arrow you have. I suspect Areel may have become a witch. Does that frighten you?"

"No, my lord. I believe in Mitra. And I can send an arrow through her heart more quickly than she can cast a spell."

"Good, good. You read my mind. Go now and accomplish this thing; return immediately, and anything you desire is yours. One arrow through the witch's heart, Hest."

"It is done already, Lord Nalor." Hest saluted, pivoted on his heel and went out.

Nalor sighed heavily and looked out the window. It was not quite dawn yet. That was well; let it all be finished in one night, and then let the lies of the day—Kus' lies, humanity's lies—provide the explanation for it when the sun glared starkly upon the world.

He was a soldier, was Hest—trained in surreptitiousness, trained in violence. Through now in the employ of a citied nobleman, he had put in his time in the field, tracking game animals, scouting captured enemy soldiers let loose in forests as part of the Zamoran war games. And, being a man, he had some practical knowledge about cities, and walls, and locks, and doors and windows. In his youth he had had to survive on the street, often stealing for food and money. Only the most resolute locks had withstood his trained tinkering.

Therefore, entering Areel's patio by the back gate,

and her apartment by the small door beside the garden, offered precious little difficulty for him. It was a little before dawn; gray tinged the air, swallows and robins stirred and chirruped, the dew was fresh on the leaf. Not even a ghost could have overheard the silent footfalls of Hest's boots on the flags of the entrance-way.

Not even a ghost . . . but perhaps a witch. . . .

Not knowing where Areel slept, Hest used his insight. He knew it was the habit of aristocracy to sleep on the second floor of their homes, so he took the stairs one flight up. He knew also that aristocrats preferred to sleep in large, airy rooms—the better to escape the summer heat. And, as he had judged from outside on the patio, he found that a spacious room occupied the far western wing of this house's second floor, overlooking the garden.

Hest stole down the hall, his footsteps still as silent as if he had been tracking a jungle cat on the moss-carpeted forest floor.

The doorway was wide and unguarded; the portals themselves, in fact, were opened, only the curtains fluttering faintly, blocking the view of the inner chamber. Hest slid past those curtains and stood, barely breathing, in the ante-chamber of the sleeping room. Surely, he realized, the ornaments and furnishings he saw in the dim light—the golden lamps and brazen statues and bookshelves full of volumes and scrolls—indicated that this was the room of the mistress of the household.

A slim door to Hest's left was the only entrance further on. He moved toward it, pulling an arrow from his quiver and nocking it on his bowstring; then, holding the bow in his left hand, he took long, long moments to unlatch the door.

It was not locked.

Vaguely, wonder grew in his brain that Areel had left her home so unguarded.

Aye; but, he reminded himself, if she were a witch, would she not suppose that that knowledge would deter would-be burglars?

He opened the door barely, just enough to let himself slide in. The chamber was shadowed; no oil lamps, and even the shutters were closed against the cool night. . . .

And there, behind the gossamer curtains surrounding the bed, lay the sleeping woman's form, barely breathing beneath soft silken covers, dark-haired head upon the pillow. Her breasts pointed up and moved softly with sleep—breasts indicating the heart that pulsed silently under flesh. . . .

Hest drew up his bow, securely nocking the arrow. The gossamer curtains would not throw off his aim—

Without pause, he loosed. The bow twanged; the arrow, steel-tipped and coated with a poison Hest had found good even against bears and buffaloes, was a blur in the air. In a heartbeat the gossamer ripped, the arrow drove into the soft form on the bed—drove in solidly, beneath the breasts—

The form did not shudder, but lay still. Then, incredibly, it seemed to waver, to dissolve.

Hest gasped. There was no sleeping form on the bed—only a pile of rumpled bedding transfixed and pinned to the mattress by an arrow. An illusion. . . .

And a woman's voice rang out: *"Fool!"*

Electrified, Hest turned to his right—

"Fool! Did you think I could be caught unawares?"

A woman—aye! White-faced, dark-haired, dressed in a white robe, moving toward him from the shadows—

Hest, stunned, dropped back, away from the woman, fear and surprise just beginning to well up in him. . . .

Not quickly enough. A soft hand brushed his wrist—and Hest felt numb, found he could not move farther back. He stared at the white-faced woman.

"Fool!" Her eyes glared with proud wrath. Was there actually a dim, yellow glow in them? "Dog! Did you think I would not expect Kus or Nalor to send enemies after me?"

Hest could not move; he could not breathe; he could only stare.

"You will return to them, then," Areel proclaimed slowly. "But not just yet. Look you, soldier. . . ." She bent to a table, took up a small gourd and removed the top of it. "Do you see this? It is charged with magical force. Did you know that I am a witch? Did that not fill you with fear when you entered this house? Or were you dreaming of the riches that your master doubtless promised you, once you had transfixed me with your arrow?"

Hest could not move, could only sweat.

Areel stepped towards him. The guardsman's eyes opened wide as she placed the opened clay gourd against his chest. "This will suck forth your soul, my soldier. Can you feel it? Ah, I know you can. You cannot scream, but I know you can feel my sorcery sucking forth your soul, commanding it to the Hells. . . ."

Wild flashes of visions, feverish, blazed in Hest's skull: demons—flames—shapes of fire lapping at his raw flesh—his own face screaming as glowing sparks crawled like hot maggots within his eyes and nose. The Hells—the Hells. . . !

He could not even scream when Areel removed the clay gourd, though it felt as if every nerve in his body were being torn apart when she did so. He shuddered; his eyes, watering, stared wide in pain and horror.

Casually Areel replaced the top on the gourd, held it up in her hand. "When I drop this, you die," she said quietly. "But first, return to Nalor and tell him what has occurred."

Hest felt his legs following the command; his bow dropped from lifeless fingers; his boots scraped on the flags. He turned and faced the curtains, walked towards them.

"Go to your master!" Areel hissed. "Let your damnation warn him of his own impending fate!"

An hour later, with dawn breaking and the merchants of Shadizar just opening their stalls in the squares, Hest returned to Lord Nalor's chambers.

Kus was not present as Nalor, standing in the company of four guards in his bathing room, saw Hest mindlessly come through the door and fix him with cold, dead eyes.

"Hest, *what—?*"

"She holds me!" croaked the soldier hollowly. "She holds my soul for the Hells, and plots for you a sorcerous death!"

"Hest, *what—?*"

"She raises the gourd even now—she smashes it! *Ayeee!*" Hest's voice became a rattling scream. "*Ayeee-eee!* Gods! Save me! My soul is doomed to the *Helllls—!*"

Then he dropped to the stone floor, writhing. Nalor looked on in horror. Within moments, however, the soldier had ceased to scream and his corpse lay motionless on the cold tiles.

Eating an apple, Sonja walked the morning streets of

Shadizar, looking for a place to stay. Her ex-landlord's last words still rankled within her—"Begone, and good riddance, slut with a sword!"—but more than that, she was worried about Sendes. The Corinthian had left an hour before dawn, promising Sonja that he would let her know where he was staying. She had tried to stop him, to talk to him—but Sendes had left quickly after telling his story. And now Sonja was afraid for him, for Sendes had many enemies: Nalor, Kus, probably Areel as well. . . .

But she could not try to follow up on Sendes until later. First she needed a place to stay; and so, walking towards the south end of the city, she inquired at every old building she came to that had a sign out advertising rooms to let.

Chost and his band dogged her footsteps. She had bought them all breakfast—fruit and cheese and wine for six young boys—and now they were chattering away behind her, offering all manner of suggestions as to places to stay.

"A friend of mine has an uncle who runs a place—"

"She don't wanna stay in your uncle's place. It's a rat trap! I bet she's got the money to afford—"

"What about them places on the other side of town?"

And so on. Sonja finally decided she needed to be rid of the urchins for an hour or two. Reaching into her purse, she drew out a gold coin—one of the few remaining to her. "See this, lads?"

Half a dozen pairs of eyes grew wide.

"Whoever finds Sendes and lets me know where he is, gets this gold piece. Fair?"

"Do you mean it?"

"Sure as Mitra watches, I mean it. Now get going. I want to find him. And don't let everyone in the city know about it, either!"

In ones and twos they ran off. Chost lingered a moment, looking back at Sonja. She replaced the gold coin and took the boy into her confidence with a wise smile. "I have to know where he is, Chost. He's in great danger."

"Aye. . . ."

"See if you can find him."

"All right, Sonja. . . ."

Sonja watched him as he ran off, then continued on her way southward through Shadizar.

It was a little before noon when she reached the squalid old apartment house by the far southern wall. The atmosphere of this end of the city did not bother her; she wished only to find some house-master who would accept gold from a sword-toting woman and give her lodging at something less than a falsely escalated price. Her money was dwindling quickly. She noticed the sign hanging in the front window—a scrawling announcement in grammatically imperfect Zamorian. Following the arrow painted on the dried sheep's hide, she walked half-way down an adjacent alley and knocked on the door. While waiting for an answer, she glanced casually at an old woman sitting on the steps.

The woman lifted a wine bottle to her mouth and took a large swallow, then wiped her lips with the back of one hand. Without looking at Sonja, she asked: "Looking for a place to stay?"

"Aye. . . ."

"Be careful that he don't give you a room on the second flight up."

"Oh? Why?"

The hag cocked a red-rimmed eye towards Sonja. "There was a witch lived up on that floor—I swear you, by Ishtar's teats!"

"Indeed."

"Oh, aye, indeed. Died just last night—murdered, I'd bet. May be that others'll tell you she died from her own witchery, but me, I thinks it was demons as did her—"

The door opened suddenly. "What is it?"

The landlord was a bloated man, blind in one eye, wearing a leather apron that stank of wine and grease and beer. Sonja faced him squarely.

"You have rooms to let?"

"I have," he grunted.

"What're you asking?"

"Three coppers a night, fifteen by the week."

"Don't you think that's a little high?"

"Three coppers a night, fifteen by the week. Take it or leave it."

"May I see a room?"

One-eye regarded her for a long moment, then pulled open the door and led the way down a rancid-smelling hall to a door on the ground floor. "It's just a room. Getcher own water from the pump out back. Have you a horse?"

"Aye."

"There's a stable out back, a copper a night."

"You must do a lucrative business."

"A copper a night for the horse."

"Does that include feeding him and letting him sleep?"

The landlord gave her a dismal look, unrelieved by any levity. "Aye. Food and sleep. A copper a night."

Sonja looked around the room; it was even more soulless than the one she'd just vacated—for three coppers a night, horse included at the stables two streets over. "I'll take it."

"As you please," muttered the fat owner, holding out his hand.

She dug into her pouch and handed over the last of her coppers, enough for two nights' stay. She had three silver minars and two gold pieces left. "Is there a key to it?"

"Lock was busted long ago. You want one put on, I'll have to charge you for it. . . ."

"Never mind."

A room found, Sonja sauntered out and went into the tavern next door to order lunch. Once she had eaten, she would hike back northward to get her horse and move it closer to her.

And somewhere along the way, she suspected, she would run into Chost or one of his band. No fear of losing them! Now that she knew that gangs of young children roamed Shadizar by day and night, she was keeping an eye out for them, and had begun to recognize many faces over and over again. The children of the street, the wastrels of civilization. . . .

It was late in the afternoon when Endithor's daughter set aside her books and turned to the jars and flasks of liquids, powders and incenses she had stolen from the witch Osumu. Events were moving quickly, and Areel knew it was necessary for her to take extreme measures to protect herself. Night would be falling shortly—and there was no telling what new peril it might bring from Nalor or Kus. Areel began to examine the incense powders, then to pour differing amounts of them into a brass brazier, following instructions in one of Osumu's books.

There was a knock on the door, and Lera entered with her mistress' afternoon wine.

"Set it on the table there, Lera. And come here."

The girl did as she was bade, hesitant. Her mistress had changed radically in the past few days. That Lord

111

Count Nalor regarded her as a potential enemy was common gossip, and some of the servants had even begun to whisper that their master's daughter was a witch. The very sleeping chamber, here, had come to seem more like a witch's haunt than the airy young noblewoman's room of a week past.

Areel paid no attention to her servant's fear and hesitation. "I want you to call all the male servants to me, Lera."

"Now, mistress?"

"Yes. Now."

Lera waited, staring as Areel mixed together the powders. Areel looked up, irritation in her gaze. "What are you waiting for?"

"Nothing, mistress."

"Then go! Order them to me, now!"

"Yes, mistress!"

More afraid then ever, Lera began to search the house for the man-servants. One by one, she alerted them to Areel's orders, wholly unable to hide the fear that clutched her.

"What does she wish, Lera? And why do you stammer so? This bird must roast—"

"Now, Zender! Leave off your cooking. She demands you *now!*"

"But, Lera," complained the groom tending the horses in the stable, "surely Mistress understands that every day I must—"

"Siloum, just do as she orders. Please!"

She found Tirs, the last one, in the kitchens, making notes of areas needing cleansing and polishing. Tirs was the oldest of them, almost like a father to Lera, a friend to the late Lord Endithor—and to Areel.

"What's troubling the mistress now?" he muttered aloud, hastening through the apartment as Lera followed at his heels. "I swear, the girl is becoming more and more strange as the days pass. Ever since my lord was taken away. . . ."

Lera followed him to the door of Areel's chamber. As Tirs entered, Areel softly began to shut the door against the maid-servant. Lera, staring fearfully into Areel's demonic cold eyes, stepped back across the hall. A strange perfume entered her nostrils; she was surprised that her mistress seemed not affected by it, for it felt to her for a moment as if her senses were being stolen from her, dreamily. . . .

But even as the door closed, there was a knocking sound at another door, and Lera hastened downstairs and through the rooms to answer it. It was the outside door, leading to the street. Nervous and agitated, Lera opened it.

A private messenger stood there—a young man, handsome, sporting a moustache. "You must be Lera," he said.

"I—yes. How did you know?"

"The sender of this said you were the only maid-servant in this house. Here." He handed her a sealed missive, and waited.

Lera tore open the letter, then looked at the messenger. "Oh—sorry. . . ." Areel kept coppers on a table by the door; Lera handed a palmful to the man.

"Thank you, miss. Good day to you."

"Good day. . . ."

Endithor had caused her to be taught how to read—had, in fact, done the same for all his servants because, in his unusual outlook, all humans deserved to know and understand whatever they could, no matter what their stations on earth. Lera now thanked all the gods, many times over, that her dear Lord Endithor had taken the pains to so instruct her—for the letter was from the Corinthian soldier, Sendes.

Lera:—I know I can trust you. Perhaps you have

heard by this time of the cruel crime your mistress
subjected me to. I am full of woe and fear. I am in
hiding, not only from Nalor but from Areel as
well. You must help me! In Mitra's holy name,
aid me if you possibly can! Please meet me
outside the city tonight. There is a group of elm
trees a hundred paces from the northwest
barbican. It is safe there. I will be watching for
you. I know I presume much by making this
request, but I beg you, in the name of Endithor,
the master you loved and the Councillor I
respected, to meet me and hear me out. I must
have justice!

                              At midnight—Sendes

Astonished, breathless, Lera held the note to her
breast, then read it again and yet again. Yes, she had to
do as Sendes asked! Yet, no—she couldn't, she
couldn't possibly. What if Areel found out? What
if—?

She read it a fourth time, stopped half-way through.
Mitra and Ishtar! What danger was Sendes in? What
insanity was her mistress brewing?

From deep within the apartment house, she heard
the door of her mistress' chamber opening. Sweating—shaking—Lera rolled up the letter, folded it,
slipped it beneath her tunic. Then she hurried down
the hallway, ran up a flight—and stopped anguished, as
she saw Tirs and the other servants of the household
coming towards her. They were walking uncertainly,
slowly, staring blankly ahead of them, looking at her
—looking *through* her, not really seeing her—

As Tirs came closer, shuffling slowly, the girl cried
out to him. "Tirs? What has—?"

"Lera!" It was her mistress' voice. She looked away,

startled. Areel was standing in the doorway to her chambers.

Lera backed towards the wall as Tirs and the others, mindless, ignoring her, walked on down the corridor, down the stairs, groping their way almost blindly.

"Come here, Lera."

She wondered that she was still alive, that she still had her mind and wits, so consumed was she with fear! "Y-yes, mistress. . . ."

"Come closer, Lera." Areel smiled.

Lera stepped forward slowly, until she was within an arm's length of her mistress.

"Are you frightened, Lera?"

"M-mistress, I. . . ."

"Of me? Of them?"

Lera could say nothing. Her throat felt dry.

"You have no reason to fear any of the servants from now on, Lera. I control them absolutely. They will protect me, and you. And there is no reason for you to fear me either, Lera."

The girl bobbed her head.

"I command powers now, Lera. Is that what frightens you? Poor child. But the servants are safe. I merely hold their souls, now—as I hold their bodies—in my own employ. They will protect us better now than they could have formerly, for they do not hunger, or thirst, or grow tired, or feel pain, or yearn for sleep. You need not fear."

"You—you will not—?"

Areel smiled again. "I will not change you. You will not breathe the incense. As long as you do my bidding, you will remain as you are. I know you will continue to serve me, as well as you always have—will you not, Lera?"

"Y-yes, Mistress."

"Of course. Remain loyal, child, and you have naught to fear. You shall be of great service to me even as my father would have wished."

"Y-yes—I will. . . ." She bobbed her head.

"You know my father was a good man, Lera, for he was good to you. Surely you must rejoice that I am now taking revenge upon those who tortured and slew him. Fate is strange. . . ." Areel's voice, soft until now, suddenly hardened. "Who was at the door?"

"A m-messenger."

"For me?"

"Y-yes. No! Well, no."

"Was there a message, Lera?"

"He had a message—but it was for an address farther up the street."

"Ah. Well, then." Areel turned to re-enter her room. "Zender will not be finishing supper tonight, Lera. I have him guarding the kitchen door. Finish preparing the meal, will you?"

"Yes, mistress."

"And if Zender asks for food, do not give him any. It may take him and the others a while to adjust—they may think that they still hunger for food—but their bodies can no longer handle it. All right? Now, run along and finish the supper for us."

Every step of the way she felt numb in body and spirit, awakened beyond herself, as if she were pinioned on a precipice with daggers of fear on one side and leaping flames of death on the other. Every step of the way she expected to be accosted by soldiers of the city patrol, or by drunkards or rapists—expected Areel to somehow find or discover her, although she knew she had left her mistress communing with dark gods in a drugged sleep induced by the black lotos. . . .

And every step of the way she expected shadows to leap at her from behind brick walls, to bear her down and rip her throat and drain her body and soul. *Ilorku. . . .*

Even when she was clear of the city gate and approaching the elm grove outside, along the road leading north, Lera feared that Sendes might not be there. He might have been killed—or, terror might have caused him to flee—or, perhaps it was all just a trick. . . .

And when a male voice called to her, in a hoarse whisper—"Lera! Thank Mitra!"—she screamed pitifully, fearful for an instant that the darkness or the trees had spoken to her, found her out and damned her.

Sendes stepped onto the grass from behind a tree. In the starlight and moonlight, his armor glinted silvery and the perspiration on his face lent him a ghostly sheen.

"Thank Mitra!" he expostulated again. "Gods, girl, come here, quickly! Are you afraid?"

She went to him; and though she barely knew Sendes, though she knew that he had been Areel's lover, she accepted the brotherly embrace of his arms, because it lent her warmth and steadied the shuddering that wracked her slim form.

"Quiet, quiet, child. You're safe. You're all right. We'll both be safe, now. We're going to stop Areel. All this terrible torture will end, now. If you'll help me. . . ."

She looked up at him—at the gray face painted with lines of moon's silver. She began to speak—

—and stopped herself.

"What? What is it?" Sendes whispered soothingly. "Tell me what you're afraid of."

She looked away from him, slipped from his arms. Her shivering anguish was past, now. "Areel—" she began, then faced Sendes once more and, as if borrowing from his purpose and strength, told him: "Today—she mystified—hypnotized—performed some kind of witchcraft on the servants of the house."

"What? Why?"

"Because of last night—Didn't you hear? Nalor, or someone, sent an assassin to slay Mistress. I suspect she slew him, instead . . . although she said she merely fogged his brain and returned him to Nalor."

"I never heard. I've been hiding in the alleys all day."

"It is true, Sendes."

He wiped his sweating face, thought a long moment. "She must be destroyed," he murmured.

"But she is still Mistress Areel!" Lera heard herself protesting. "Only a week ago—only days ago—she was my mistress, she was not some witch, not this—this—"

"She is mad! I think she has sold her soul to dark powers in order to avenge her father. She's evidently willing to sacrifice anyone to achieve that goal. How do you know she doesn't plan to sacrifice *you*—to finish what her father attempted? Did you ever think of that? And you would weaken, and falter, and not try to defend yourself against her simply because three or four days ago she was Endithor's daughter, and *not* a mistress of Hell?"

Astonished at herself, Lera made no comment other than: "Tell me what you want me to do. I can't promise that I'll do it—all I want is to run away—escape—although I fear she'd find me with her sorcery. . . ."

"When we've done what we must, Lera, there'll be no need to run and escape. There'll be nothing to escape from. Except, perhaps, Nalor and Kus. But Areel, I think, is the cause of their anger. . . ."

"Tell me what you want me to do."

He led her to a flat-topped rock behind some elms and sat her down beside him. "I don't want to put you in any more danger than you're already in, Lera. But if it's dangerous for you to live in Areel's house, doing nothing, then it's no more dangerous for you to be acting in your own defense.

"All I want you to do, for now, is to win Areel's confidence. Are you afraid of Nalor? Of Kus? No—no—you don't even know them. But they are Areel's enemies—they have attacked her house—so beg her for protection. Tell her you're afraid, that you don't want to die, that you need her, that you'll do anything to help her. That's the first step. If she'll permit it, stay with her when she works her sorcery. Tell her you're afraid to be alone, or that you're afraid of the servants—anything. If she thinks you're frightened enough—and dependent enough upon her—she may be vain enough not to mind. I know Areel, how vain and proud she is. Make sure she trusts you, Lera; and when you're sure, go into her room and try to find the things most important to her—any implements of magic, but especially the most important ones. Take them and hide them. Give them to me later. When Areel finds them gone, claim that Kus or Nalor's guards entered and ransacked the place. Do you understand?"

"Yes, yes. . . ." Lera was breathless.

"Take those magical things and bring them to me. I am hiding on the Street of the Wine-merchants, down on the southeast side of town. You know where that is? Yes? Then ask at the Sign of the Unicorn for me. The master there is a crafty Aquilonian; he knows me by the name of Ombus. All right? Ombus."

"Ombus. . . ."

"Bring the articles to me. Do it within a day or two, all right?"

"Yes, yes. . . ."

"Because when you do it, I have one more thread to add to the knot, and then we'll have her. Understand?"

"Yes, Sendes, yes."

"She must be destroyed."

Lera didn't say anything.

"Aren't you afraid of her? Don't you want her dead?"

"I—I just want her to go away. I want to be able to go away myself—and be safe. Without—being pursued by sorcery. . . ."

"You'll be safe. We'll both be safe. We'll be able to leave Shadizar without worrying about Areel and her witchcraft any longer. Now, what's my name?"

"Sen—Ombus. Ombus."

"At the Sign of the Unicorn."

"At the Sign of the Unicorn."

Sendes stood up, sighed heavily, stretched. "Come. I'll see you back through the city safely, Lera."

Her eyes were set, reflecting the shimmering moonlight.

"In a day or two, Lera, in three days at most, we'll be free of her."

She bobbed her head. "Yes, I know. . . ." But she could not quite believe him.

Chapter 6.

As Sendes watched, Lera made her way through the low foliage of the rear garden and approached a side door of the apartment. She paused beneath an oil lamp to fit her key into the lock, then turned and waved to the young soldier.

Safe.

Sendes watched her go inside and close the door silently behind her. Then he moved away from the gate and walked rapidly down the street, breathing more easily. Lera was safely home. He did not fear any attack from anyone; he, also, would be safely home very soon. And Lera, he hoped—he trusted—would begin to put their plan into effect. For the moment, he was content—not happy, but less like a driven man, a haunted man. He felt securer, more like himself, now that he was fighting back, or beginning to fight back.

His pace quickened down the cobbles. No soldiers passed him on the way, no drunkards or bandits barred his path, no *ilorku* lurked in the shadows.

But other eyes did, indeed, watch him.

As he turned a corner and hurried down a side-street, small feet pattered quickly over the cobbles, following. Sendes did not hear them; and if he had, he would not have thought much of seeing a young, tow-headed street urchin wandering alone in the avenues of Shadizar, late at night.

Tirs was standing guard in the kitchen.

Still and silent he stood, absolutely motionless, pale as a lich in the dully reflected moonlight streaming through the side windows. Lera saw him, and hesitated.

"Tirs?"

His eyes were on her, but he did not move, did not utter her name.

Cautiously, Lera approached, a graceful shadow moving through hard, sinister shadows. "Don't you recognize me, Tirs?" She walked slowly up to him, stood directly before him. He tilted his head downward, looked at her with empty eyes—eyes vacant of any intelligence or recognition.

"You don't even know me any more, do you, Tirs?" Lera whispered. One silver tear began to run down her cheek.

She moved to walk past him. A shift in the night—one of Tirs' hands clasped on Lera's forearm. She pivoted, fear blossoming in her heart, staring at him.

"Tirs? Don't you know me? It's me—Lera. Oh, Tirs. . . ."

For a moment he stared blankly at her. Then the hand released her; Tirs turned away, watched the door of the kitchen.

Still sobbing quietly, Lera hastened on through the apartment toward her own quarters, which were down the hall from the kitchen. As she went in, she listened for sounds of any disturbance above her, for Mistress Areel's chamber was situated directly overhead. Faintly, Lera could sense the lingering aroma of the heady black lotos. Assuming that Areel was fast asleep in a drugged fantasy, she quietly undressed and crawled into her bed.

But she could not sleep. For perhaps an hour she fidgeted restlessly, listening for sounds in the night that did not come, hearing Sendes' warning words over and over again in her mind. When at last she heard the distant tolling of temple gongs marking the third hour after midnight, she sat up and lit a candle, drew her knees up to her breasts, wrapped her arms around her legs and sat, thinking.

Thinking, and listening.

Listening, for—what? Her own fear?

Gradually, she began to nod off to sleep. . . .

Until a sound—yes, above her!—brought her back.

She did not know the time. Her candle had not melted much. Quietly, she stretched out her legs and listened attentively, following the footsteps as they paced the chamber above. They could be no one's but Areel's. There was the sound of a door opening, then the footsteps hurrying down the stairs and pattering away, and finally—faintly—an echo of a sound of the outside doors opening and closing.

And that was all.

Lera half-started from her bed, wondering where her mistress had gone—then thought better of her curiosity. Better, perhaps, not to know. . . .

Again unable to sleep, she retrieved Sendes' original note from beneath her pillow and re-read it, read it once more, and remembered his words to her in the grove. It was so—spontaneous, so chancy. How could they ever hope to trap or slay Areel? Areel, with her magic. . . .

"*. . . when you're sure, go into her room and try to find the things most important to her. Any implements of magic . . .*"

Now. . . .

Now, while Areel was gone—while there was an opportunity to do it and get it done, and then flee—escape—get away from this madness forever. . . .

Lera was dressed in her light chiton, out of the room, up the stairs and at Areel's door before the audacity of her decision really struck her. Even then, on the threshold of her mistress' deeply shadowed den of witchcraft, she cautioned herself, calmed herself, but did not back away. It must be done. The sheer boldness of doing it gave her courage, where the plotting of it and anticipation of it had brought to her only doubt and fear.

She knew the room by heart, having served her mistress in it daily for over four years. There was a lamp lit, the one on the table by the bed. From a stand by the door Lera took up another oil lamp and a wooden match, lit the match at the first lamp and with it the lamp in her hand. Then she began to circuit the room slowly, looking at the numerous old books on the shelves, the trinkets, amulets, phials, jars and instruments. She knew not what to make of any of them. Grotesque, full of uncanny presentiments, they filled her with worry and trepidation. *Any implements of magic.* . . . But what could she take, what could she hide, that might reduce her power enough to—

A sudden noise.

Mitra! Had Areel returned so soon?

Grabbing up a few symbol-inscribed ornaments, Lera turned from a shelf case, went to place her oil lamp on a table, and in turning faced the window.

Something was there, disturbing the moonlight—black, flowing, like a living shadow. But not silent like a shadow, for it made clacking, gravelly noises, and it was coming through the window. . . !

Lera screamed.

The twin panes of the window burst open with a crash. Outlined by the moonlight, tall and insubstantial in the gloom, the black thing arose and wavered—cascaded—took on a more solid shape—

Lera screamed and screamed. She dropped the oil lamp. Flames burst up on the wooden floor.

Then came the sound of running footsteps, from downstairs—Tirs and the others, coming—

The menacing black shadow coalesced in the moonlight, hardened within the orange glow of the oil lamp and the skittering flames. It took shape: a body, tall and lean—two eyes, glaring, yellow—a hissing, white-fanged mouth—

Into Areel's chamber burst Tirs and Siloum and the other four servants, hastening on shuffling feet.

There was a tall, dark-robed man by the window, standing erect, yellow eyes gleaming, red mouth agape in a sinister grin. He surveyed the room calmly, ignoring the flames, then made an imperious gesture. The servants halted. Lera cringed in fear.

"Stay back!" he commanded. Then he looked upon Lera. "Where is Areel?"

"She—she is not here. Gods!" Her voice seemed to her an echo; her body was trembling, numb, coated with icy perspiration.

"Not here? Tell me, then, where she is!"

Lera stared, gaping. The oil flames, dying out at her feet, nearly caught at the hem of her chiton; she jumped back, fell against the shelves, bumping herself painfully.

"Tell me where she is, girl."

"Who are you?" Lera screamed, shutting her eyes, then opening them again to the horror. *"What are you?"*

The lean man lifted his head high. "I am Kus," he

announced, the name slithering from his lips. "Kusss—and I am come to destroy Areel. Tell me where to find her!"

Lera nearly swooned, caught hold of the shelves, tried to think what she might do, how she might escape. . . .

Tirs attacked first; the others fell in behind him. They moved lumberingly, and Kus laughed at them as they approached.

"Mindless!" His voice was a roar of unholy mirth. "Soulless! Trapped by sorcery! Die in the Hells, fools!"

With one hand he grabbed Tirs by the throat and lifted him from the ground. Tirs' boots kicked. Siloum, charging from the other side, raised his fists to strike. The sorcerer clutched for him with his other hand; talon-like nails ripped into flesh, and Siloum fell back, voiceless, an arc of blood spurting from his torn throat.

Kus, hissing, pulled Tirs to him. Lera saw the red mouth opening wide, the sharp teeth gleaming in the lamplight. Then, quick as a striking cobra, Kus buried his face in Tirs' neck. The servant kicked, but still Kus held him off the floor, neck bent back as if about to snap. A stream of blood shot free, and Lera saw with horror that Kus' throat was working up and down as he pressed his mouth to Tirs' neck. . . .

She pushed herself away from the shelves. The other servants fell upon Kus, who turned to face them with hollow, horrible laughter. Lera screamed madly, was dimly aware of herself rushing through Areel's chamber door and out into the hall—

And then blackness overtook her. Whether she stumbled or whether her mind gave way she did not know as she fell forward, skidded on her belly, and sank into unconsciousness.

* * *

Chost sat crouched for a long time after watching Sendes disappear into the Sign of the Unicorn. He knew he should go tell Sonja, but he was hungry, and he hoped that if he waited awhile he might be able to break into the Unicorn and steal some bread or cheese.

But the lamplight on the top floor of the building glowed on—and on—and was not extinguished; and Chost, not wishing to chance being discovered by a wakeful landlord or tenant, decided finally out of desperation to go to Sonja's. He knew where she was, for he had met Stiva earlier, and Stiva had already discovered the Hyrkanian's new apartment and reported to her his failure to find Sendes. So Chost knew where to find Sonja.

Sonja, and the gold piece that would buy him more bread and cheese than he could devour, even at this hungry hour. . . .

Getting into the ramshackle old building had not been difficult for Areel. She had moved quietly as a ghost, and had not betrayed herself. Silently as a shadow she had moved up the back stairs to Osumu's room in the apartment house. Here, she knew, she would find the talisman—the amulet of power, mentioned in her father's diary and in some of Osumu's old books—the talisman that would possibly effect the defeat of Nalor and Kus.

Osumu must have hidden it; Areel knew she must find it.

She needed no light to find her way about, for her witch's sense, grown stronger day by day, showed her the way. All things emit vibrations, essences, feelings—and so powerful a talisman as Areel sought was bound to radiate a keen, sharp essence. She relied upon her heightened senses to find it.

Quickly she moved about the apartment, running her hands over walls and furniture. All had been emptied; the house-master, no doubt, had already sold all the old witch's belongings for good sums to merchants in the city. But this talisman, Areel hoped, he had not sold.

So powerful a weapon Osumu must have hidden well. She would surely not have left it just lying about, or even sealed in a box somewhere. Her father's diaries had mentioned that he had only once seen it, and had heard Osumu say that she kept it well-hidden.

Well-hidden. . . . But where?

As she crossed the front room, heading for an ante-chamber, Areel felt something brush against her foot—not something alive, but a sensation, a prickly coldness—something not of this mundane sphere—

She stooped to the floor, ran her hands over the hardwood boards. . . .

Here! Here! It radiated ephemeral heat and cold; it emitted strange sensations Areel had come to recognize as part only of sorcerous things.

Here!

With a strength beyond that usual to a beautiful young noblewoman, Areel dug her fingernails into the seams of the hardwood floor, felt for the jamb of an opening—a trap door.

The door creaked loudly as she pulled it upward. . . .

While, just beneath that door, on the other side of the rafters and boards that formed the floor of old Osumu's apartment, was the ceiling of Red Sonja's apartment—and when she woke to hear thumpings and creakings and footsteps above her, she presumed the worst.

"More trouble from Kus or Nalor," she muttered. "The damned devils or some of their hirelings, creeping around up there—"

Quietly she slipped on her boots and mail tunic, pulled free her sword, opened her door and went down the hallway, then sidled up the stairs to the second floor while holding against the railing. Finally, taking a deep breath, she abandoned stealth; with a few quick steps she was outside the door of the upstairs apartment.

The groaning and cracking of wood ceased.

Sonja heard bootsteps, moving towards her within the room. The door opened, and there was a fluttery show of dark robe. Sonja jumped before the open portal, sword out.

"Hold where you stand, dog!"

Then, astonishment. Not a soldier, but a woman confronted her—and not any woman, but Endithor's daughter.

"Areel—?"

"Get away!" Areel hissed. "Get out of this door!"

But Sonja stepped ahead, sword out. "Tell me what the hell you think you're doing, snooping around here!"

Areel drew away, turned and ran across the room, then backed against a closed window.

"You're Areel sin Endithor!" Sonja charged her. "Tell me what in Mitra's name you're doing here?" Then she noticed the gleaming object in the woman's hand—an object she had thought to be an oil lamp. "What's that—?"

"I'll tell you nothing, Hyrkanian! Get away from that door!"

"Witch! Answer me, or I'll call—!"

"Call upon your ancestors!" Areel screamed, lifting her hand. In its palm the glowing object she held gleamed more brightly. Its brilliance blinded Sonja momentarily; she began to weaken, felt her knees giving way—

"Damn you!" She fell to one side, felt a resurgence of strength. Instantly, instinctively, her left hand dropped to her thigh, pulled free her side-knife and in a sweeping arc threw it in an overhand. Areel snarled and jumped back.

The knife thudded into the wooden shutters, and in the same instant the room went dark.

From downstairs began to rise the rumblings of an awakened household. Sonja leaped up and, sword out, ran forward. Areel yanked open the shutters and jumped onto the stone sill.

Sonja yelled as Areel leaped into the moonlit night, the cloth of her black robe flapping in the air as she dropped.

Carrying through with the move she'd begun, Sonja swiped; her blade dug into the wood of the window-frame.

"Damn! She moves faster than a bat—!"

Suddenly she felt a rock or pebble under her boot—something that glimmered metallically. She stooped to retrieve it.

It was the talisman.

"She dropped it!" muttered Sonja. Swiftly she snatched it up and thrust it into her belt-pouch, then leaned out the window with bared sword to see where Areel had escaped. But there was no shadow or night-movement of any sort in the street below.

She turned at the sound of bodies in the open doorway behind her.

"What the hell is going on?"

"Mitra! It sounded like an army up here!"

"Jos, ask her what the hell—!"

The house-master, and his patrons. Jos, the fat, one-eyed landlord, stepped ahead into the room, blocking Sonja's path should she decide to rush him. "What in the hell is going on here?" he demanded again.

"I don't know," Sonja told him honestly. "A burglar, I think. I heard noises from below. It was a woman. . . ."

"A woman?"

"Aye, a woman. She was here, but she jumped from the window. Got away."

"A woman burglar?"

"In this room!" Sonja told him; then, remembering her unsheathed sword, she sheathed it. "She was here, Jos. Someone was here—if not a woman, then maybe a demon with a woman's form and voice. Anyhow, she's gone now, and she couldn't have taken anything. There's nothing here to take."

Jos let out a long, dissatisfied sigh. "All right, all right. I don't know what the hell is going on, but all you people get back to your rooms. You, too, Hyrkanian. Get going."

"Aye, aye. . . ." the patrons muttered.

Under the landlord's suspicious eye, Sonja moved from the room, took the stairs down to her own room—

—And there, on the bed, pulled free the talisman, held it and examined it. It was a strangely-designed object, of a silvery metal but heavier than silver, inset with dark gems and bits of bone or ivory—a sorcerous amulet of some sort. Its design vaguely suggested some sort of reptilian monster twisted into the form of a symbol representing infinity or the Ultimate. As Sonja gazed at it, she almost felt a stirring in her mind, as of some hazy memory. . . .

And it had glowed in Areel's hand.

Was the power Areel's? Or the talisman's?

Sonja settled back, holding onto it. Now she had a card to play, a good pair of dice to throw—an entry ticket into this convoluted, indecipherable game that involved a nobleman's daughter, a nobleman's enemy and another nobleman's soldier-guard. And a sorcerer. And—Mitra knew what else!

Sonja held the talisman in her hand, and watched it. Just metal, gems, bone—with a queer feel to it, and a subtle suggestion of age. Somehow, Sonja knew, it was old, perhaps incredibly old. . . .

And Areel would be back to get it. Sometime.

But—was its power Areel's, or its own?

Lera awoke upon a divan in her mistress' room, dazed and confused—but alive. Alive.

Coming to full awareness with gasps and shudders, she lifted her hands to her throat, and felt no blood.

"Now, what in the name of the Hells happened here?" came Areel's sharp demand.

Lera turned to look at her mistress, who stood in the middle of the shattered room. She saw fallen book-cases, six ugly corpses, broken lamps and ornaments, the open window—

The window!

But no shadow there, now. Only the first gray of dawnlight coming through.

Lera shuddered, sobbed thickly, curled up on the divan and turned her face from Areel. "It didn't get me!" she sobbed into the cushions. "Oh, Mitra. Oh, Hotath! Gods, gods, gods! It didn't get me!"

Areel approached her. "Drink this."

Tearful, Lera looked up at her.

"Wine. Drink it. Then tell me what happened."

Lera sipped some of the wine, but it tasted bitter and she rejected it. Areel set the cup on a table.

"Now, Lera, tell me." Her voice sounded friendlier. "What happened here? How did these servants die? And, why were you clutching several of my magical charms when I found you unconscious?"

"Il-ilorku, mistress!"

"What?"

Lera's mind began to work in spite of her fear. *"Ilorku!* I—I heard a noise, mistress. I came up here, and it—it came in the window. Gods! It was horrible! The servants couldn't stop it. I fell against the shelves—grabbed the amulets there—"

"That may be what saved you," Areel mused. "They have power to ward off some forms of evil. If the thing that came here really was an *ilorku—*"

"Gods, mistress! It was Kus!"

"Kus!"

"Oh, Mitra—Mitra—!" Lera looked up at her; her fingers, trembling, sought to attach themselves to Areel's robe, as if to cling there for security.

"It was Kus! Kus! I heard a crash—came in—Tirs and—and the others tried to fight him—but he—he—!"

She fell back with a series of convulsive sobs, letting go of Areel and sinking into the bed.

"Oh, gods, gods! It was horrible! It was a dream—a mad dream! It couldn't have happened. *Ilorku—!"*

"Sh. Shh-hhh, Lera. . . ." Areel gently stroked the girl's blond head and looked around the room with cold eyes that held no wonder.

"And you're certain it was Sendes?" Sonja asked Chost.

They had not been talking; they had already been through this two hours ago, when Chost had thrown pebbles at Sonja's window, and she had opened the shutters to let the lad climb in. What was he doing here this late at night? Where had he been? Did he see anything of Areel?

Sonja had fed him cheese and wine—all that she had—and between swallows, Chost had told her everything: of loitering near the taverns in the Street of the Wine-Merchants late in the evening, and of seeing the furtive Sendes in his armor hurry through the town. He had followed, hoping to make sure it was indeed Sendes, had seen him go through the northwest gate, and had decided against following—too much chance of being discovered. But shortly thereafter a very young woman had exited the gate, and soon after that both she and Sendes had returned by the same route. Chost had followed them, and for a moment had a chance at good identification when Sendes and the girl passed close beneath a street torch. The girl had returned fo Lord Endithor's house, and then Sendes had returned to the Unicorn.

The room was graying with the first light of dawn when the lad finally relaxed on the floor at Sonja's bedside, lay back with his arms under his head and listened to the soothing sounds of his full stomach.

Now Sonja sat on her bed, untired after the night's excitement, and studied the talisman on its chain. She asked Chost: "You're certain it was Sendes?"

"Yes, Sonja. It was him." He sat up. "What's that thing?"

"A talisman of some kind."

"Let me see it."

She dropped it to him; Chost scrutinized it.

"Ever see anything like it?"

The lad shook his head. "No, no. . . . but it has a queer feel to it, don't it?"

"Aye. It's sorcerous."

With a mild yelp Chost threw it back to Sonja, and made a face. "Sorcerous! Don't let it near me!"

"It can't do you any harm."

"Ishtar!" he swore. "Sorcery. . . . Where did you find it?"

"A burglar broke into the room above mine last night. While you were out following Sendes."

"A burglar?"

"Aye—a woman. It was Areel, Lord Endithor's daughter. I found her and chased her. She dropped this."

"Ishtar!"

Sonja twirled the talisman on its chain. "I'm beginning to think that this might tie everything together, Chost. I think this damn little trinket just might prove to be Sudikar's Orm. I used to hear a legend, among the people of the Vilayet coast, that an ancient king named Sudikar used a talisman like this to paralyze his enemies with terror." Sonja looked down at Chost, whose eyes were closed. "There's been an awful lot of hell-raising going on in this town lately, Chost. Tired?"

He nodded. "On the streets all night, and now—with a full belly. . . ."

Sonja got out of bed. "Come on." She patted the cushions. "Get some rest."

Chost stood up. "And what about you?"

She slipped the talisman back into her belt-pouch. "I'm going to look for Sendes."

"Do you want me to come—?"

"I want you to get some sleep, Chost. Because I think things are starting to move very quickly. I may have to depend on you. And your friends."

"All right. . . ."

"If you wake up before I get back—" She drew a gold coin from her pouch.

But Chost began having second thoughts. "Keep it, Sonja."

"I made a bargain. Whoever found Sendes got the gold coin."

"Keep it. If I need it later, I'll ask you for it. In the meantime—you've given me enough food and drink and—friendship—so far. A gold coin's worth." He smiled, a curiously shy smile.

Sonja returned the grin. "All right, then. When you need it. . . ." She put it back in her purse, again urged Chost to get some rest, and went out.

Chapter 7.

Nalor sat at his table, alone. Gray dawnlight was illuminating the cracks and patterns of the mosaic tile floor of his study. The atmosphere of the chamber still seemed charged with the tense exchange Nalor had just had with Kus:

"You could not find her? Wizard! Vampire! Where is your magic? She must be destroyed before—!"

"Fool! Be silent, Nalor, lest you be next to fall to my wrath. There is yet tomorrow night, or the next night. Tend to your own duties. See that you do not botch them, nor even think to try to take over mine. You are losing your grip, Nalor. Do not offend me, or I will drink *your* blood, I will damn *your* soul."

Now, pondering, Nalor feared that Kus was correct. He was losing—something. Control. Power. He should have sensed it earlier, should have guessed that it might have happened, when Kus had originally come to him months ago with his offers of special favors, his insinuations that he could raise Nalor to kingship—if Nalor would but reciprocate and aid Kus with his own special needs.

Suddenly he felt anxious, out of control, nearly powerless. Aye, he had committed many large crimes—but, how could he have foreseen which special crime might be the one of his undoing? How could any man, living a life of action and decision, come to know in any way but hindsight which action or decision might prove to be his success or his downfall? Even seers could not predict as much.

Nalor shook his head angrily and gulped some wine. He could not blame himself—but he could blame others. He knew the old adage—"A man happy accepts all responsibility; a man sad rejects all blame"—but such banalities did not apply here. Kus was to blame. Kus—sorcerer, schemer, demon. *Ilorku.* How long had the devil been walking the earth, journeying from city to city, nation to nation from the early mists of time till now, cajoling and pleasing, tempting and corrupting with his promises of power and gold and greatness? Promising—while sucking dry the vitality of his victims, causing reality to dissipate into tormented memories, and dreams to become tinged with nightmare?

Kus!

And so another card was played from the deck, another pair of dice rolled in the game. Nalor against Kus. . . .

"The hunter who sets too many traps," ran another old adage, "may forget where one is hidden, and fall into it himself."

But the hunter trapped, Nalor reminded himself, knows the nature of the trap, whereas the imprisoned beast does not.

Dawn in Shadizar. Birds were fluttering from roosts on temples high above the city, wooden cart wheels were clattering down the cobblestones. Doors were opening, shutters swinging wide, lamps and torches being extinguished. Drunkards were slouching away into alleys, whores moving indoors, shopkeepers displaying wares, the patrols of the night changing places with those of the day. Temple bells sounded out, calling believers to prayer; city gongs rang, calling the municipal workers to their toil. And, this morning, thunderclouds were gathering high above, encroaching upon the early light of dawn and beginning to scatter raindrops upon the brick and cobblestones, the bells and the gongs and the window shutters—a fragrant drizzle, a soothing rain, soaking up some of the heat, washing away some of the dust and filth from the alleys.

Sonja walked south along the Street of the Wine-Merchants. She had been down here once before, but never to the Unicorn, which was farther along than the taverns and restaurants she had frequented. It sat rather isolated, with a razed building to its east and an untended fodder field behind it, near the south wall of Shadizar. The front door was opened for business.

A thin old woman was standing behind the counter, mopping up. Sonja entered, her boots sounding on the rough wooden boards. She took a table; the thin old woman eyed her suspiciously, finally came around.

"What will you be having this morning?"

Sonja ordered a plate of eggs and some light ale. The old woman went to the kitchen.

As Sonja's vision adjusted to the dimness of the room, she saw a man seated at a table near the opposite wall. He was a small man with a drawn face, well-dressed, and his steady gaze continued upon Sonja, measuring her. She watched him.

After a moment, the man made a subtle gesture; he wiped his left eye, as though to remove the sleep from it. Sonja recognized the move; he was an informer—a spy—a denizen of the streets who specialized in keeping eyes and ears open, then selling information for whatever gold or silver he could get. His kind was familiar to Sonja—part of the criminal underground of Shadizar, and all cities.

He waited after making his gesture.

Sonja scratched her throat, the fleshy area between her collarbones, then sat back. There was a clatter of pans in the kitchen.

Casually, smiling knowingly, the informer stood up and crossed the room, took a chair opposite Sonja at her table.

"Good morning," he grinned.

"Good morning."

"And may we be of help?"

"Perchance," Sonja answered slowly. "It depends on the price."

The informer smiled. "Quibbling." His eyes roamed languidly over Sonja's womanly form. "We can decide on a price later. Depends on many things."

"I'm looking for a soldier."

"City, royal or private?"

"Private employ."

The informer's eyes lit up. "All right. Who is he, what's he done, where's he been? And how long ago?"

"He's one of Lord Nalor's guards."

The informer pursed his lips; Sonja read the subtle shades of knowledge in his face. "This will cost a bit."

"Where is he?"

"The most powerful noble in Shadizar has many—"

"Don't play games with me, dog." Sonja said it levelly, with just a hint of threat.

"Has he a name?"

"Sendes."

"I may know him, but he doesn't go by that name."

"No doubt he doesn't. I want to know what room he's in."

"It seems you know a lot already." The informer watched Sonja carefully, then leaned across the table. "Let's see the color of your gold."

Sonja leaned back a bit—as if reaching for her purse. Then, without warning, she was on her feet, kicking her chair back against the wall, lifting and shoving the table against the informer. He squawked as he was thrown back, still in his chair, and pinned to the ground by the heavy oaken board which crushed onto his chest. Sonja stepped around the table, her sword slithering out, its point moving forward to just press upon the informer's soft throat.

Shocked and surprised, barely able to breathe, he looked up with eyes full of horror. "What—in the Hells are—you doing—?"

"What room is he in?" Sonja whispered.

"Snail. Snail-room. . . ."

"This is the color of my gold," Sonja hissed, pricking the dog's throat with her blade. "Now get up."

She stood back, watching as the man rolled the table aside and got to his feet, gasping and coughing. Again she touched him with the point of her sword, causing him to back against the wall.

"A word of warning," Sonja hissed at him. "My payment to you is that I won't slit your throat. And don't think to go running to get your friends, either. If I ever see your face again, I'll turn it to stone. See this?"

She removed the talisman from her belt-pouch and dangled it before the informer's white, fear-frozen face.

"Do you recognize it?"

"Mitra! You're a witch!"

"I'll twist your soul every direction but one," Sonja promised him, "if I ever see you again. You never saw me—you never saw that dog of a nobleman's guard—do you understand?"

It was all clear to the informer. Sendes had committed some offense against Nalor, and Nalor—the most powerful noble in the city—had employed this strange woman, half sword-adept and half witch, to find him out.

"Do—you—understand?" Sonja asked between tight teeth.

"Gods, yes!" he gasped. "I'll say nothing, I swear!"

She drew back her blade, pocketed the talisman again. "Then get out of here. One word about this, and I'll damn you to the Hells."

"Mitra, I am gone! I am the wind!" Stumbling, fearful, he hurried out of the tavern.

Sonja hid her smile. She may have saved Sendes from discovery; at least, the informer might now be less ready to blab his knowledge into dangerous ears.

She sheathed her sword, pivoted on her heel—and faced the lean old woman, who stood, silent and gray, near the overturned table, a plate of steaming eggs in her hands.

Sonja glowered at her. "The same goes for you! You don't know who I am, you never saw me."

The old woman bobbed her head. Her eyes were cold, her face expressionless. She seemed like one used to keeping silence.

"The room of the snail. Is it upstairs?"

A frail hand pointed to a door across the room.

Sonja stalked across the boards, opened the door and went up, scowling to herself. It seemed one had an advantage in this mad, fear-crazed town, if one aligned oneself with the fear. . . .

The door with the snail painted on it was at the end of the hall. Sonja rapped on the wood. There was no response from within. She rapped again, harder.

"Open up, Sendes!"

Footsteps sounded. "Mitra! Who is it?" She could hear the rasp of his blade being drawn.

"Red Sonja, you stupid fool! Open the door!"

It opened a bit; an eye looked out. Then the door was opened fully.

"How did you find me?"

Sonja stepped in, closed the door behind her, regarded the Corinthian carefully. "That's a story in itself. Put up your sword. You don't need it—yet."

Sendes sheathed his weapon. "How in Mitra's name did you find me, Sonja?"

"I'll get to that. For the moment—have you anything for breakfast?"

"Just some wine."

"That'll have to do. I'm afraid my eggs have been fed to the dogs by this time. Now—thank you," she said as Sendes handed her the bottle. "I'm afraid I caused something of a commotion, coming up here. I don't think anyone will bother you presently, but you never can tell."

"Sonja, what's happening? How did you find me? Does Nalor know—?"

"Not a thing, as far as I can tell. But you'd better think about removing to another rooming house. Men on the run can't stay in one place for too long."

"I can't move," he replied quietly. "I must wait here."

"For what? For Areel's maid-servant?"

He looked at her, eyes wide and full of questions.

"I know a few things," Sonja told him, "but not everything. I want to talk to you, because an awful lot happened last night. We'd better start putting the pieces into place."

"What about Lera? Sonja?"

She shrugged, handed Sendes the wine bottle. "As I

143

say, let's start putting the pieces together, before we're all damned to the Hells. If I'm going to be fighting vampires and sorcerers and witches in this damned town, then by Tammuz, I'm going to find out why!"

The house still stank of the six corpses burnt at dawn. Lera sensed the peculiar odor of human flesh burned, not by ordinary fire, but by magical flames—flesh, bones and souls destroyed all at once, leaving no trace. It was a lingering odor, evil and undefined, made horrible by its association with sorcerous death.

She had to get away—get out of this house, even if only for a while.

After the incineration of the bodies, Areel had voiced her intention to retire for a few hours. Lera timidly spoke to her of going out to get some needed food for the kitchen, and Areel let her go. Taking her basket with her, the girl appropriated some of the coppers from the table by the front door, then hired a one-horse carriage to take her to the Street of the Wine-merchants. Sendes' letter she bore within her vest. When she got out of the carriage she paid the driver three coppers; then, side-stepping puddles and wiping drizzle-dampened hair from her eyes, she made her way into the Unicorn.

There were a few patrons within: ruffians, hard-eyed women, soldiers in outlander uniforms. Lera was bait for their eyes. Shopping basket still in hand, the young maid-servant approached the counter and looked at the thin old woman behind.

The old woman, frowning, came up to her. "What is it?"

In a whisper: "I'm looking for a friend of mine. Ombus?"

The old woman paled. "Who?"

"His name is Ombus," Lera repeated, frightened at the possibilities suggested by the old woman's reaction. "What room is he in?"

"Snail. Through that door, there. Second floor."

"Thank you." A sweet smile, and Lera crossed the room.

The old woman watched her go; then her eyes roved around the tavern. By Hotath!—if witchcraft were to take place in her house, could any of these rascals be able to help—?

Lera found the room and rapped timidly on the door. "Ombus?" she called out in a low voice. "Ombus?"

The door opened. Sendes stood before her, gray and haggard; behind him, sitting against the farther wall, was a red-haired woman wearing a sleeveless shirt of mail. Lera looked from one of them to the other.

"Come in," Sendes said softly, taking Lera's hand, then closing the door. "Come in. You never met Red Sonja, did you?" He turned to the woman. "Sonja—Lera, Areel's maid."

"How do you do, Lera?" Sonja did not rise, but watched the girl carefully.

"Come, Lera—" Sendes motioned to what was left of the wine. "Sit. Have something to drink."

"No, thank you."

Sonja waved a hand. "Aye—sit, girl. We want to hear your side of this. We're trying to piece it all together, you see—so we can decide what we're going to do next. . . ."

An hour later, with the wine gone and the weather outside keeping up its ceaseless drizzle, the aggregate facts were laid plain, and a path of action had been cautiously proposed. There was Nalor and Kus on the one side—Kus, the vampire, the sorcerer, to some extent holding Nalor in his grasp. On the other side was

Areel, working for vengeance against Nalor for her father's death. She had decided to use sorcery; how she had gained her knowledge of it was unclear, but that she was now a sorceress was obvious. Those facts given, the recent events played themselves out like pieces on a game-board; Areel had bewitched Sendes and tried to have him slay Nalor; that failing, Nalor had reacted by sending an assassin against Areel; the assassin, failing in turn, had left the apartment without harming Areel. Sendes, having to go into hiding, had contacted Lera last night about a plan to get even with Areel—who had, that same night, broken into the apartment above Sonja's for some unknown reason.

"I think this magic amulet had something to do with it," Sonja commented. "Areel might have gained her sorcery from whoever lived in that room earlier. I was told a witch lived on that floor. So—last night was indeed a night of strange events! One of my street urchins followed you two—and Kus, attempting to succeed where Nalor had failed, came last night to attack Areel. Areel being absent, he attacked you, Lera, and the six controlled servants who guarded the house of Endithor's daughter. All the pieces fit."

"Except," Sendes reminded her grimly, "where we go from here." He looked at Lera. "You're still willing to help me fight Areel?"

She nodded briskly.

Sonja suggested: "Why don't you just leave Shadizar? You're only endangering yourselves by staying here."

"Because no matter how far I might travel, Sonja, there would be a price on my head. Nalor would make certain of that. I could not risk it. I must lie low, at least for a time yet."

"And you, Lera?" Sonja looked at the girl.

The maid-servant averted her eyes. "Areel would find me—kill me—with her magic. I fear she intends to sacrifice me, in a ritual against Kus, like—like the one her father attempted. . . ."

"But, Sonja, you're not really a part of this," Sendes cautioned her.

"I am now. Did you know Kus found out where I roomed, shortly after I confronted him at the feast? He and some guards were lurking about at night, watching. I hope my change of quarters threw them off."

"Have you seen them since?" Sendes asked uneasily.

"No. But I'm sure their intentions were sinister, and that Kus has not given up."

Sendes relaxed a bit. "Kus was piqued, I'm sure. But I doubt that either he or Nalor are concerned about you any more. All they wish is Areel, dead. And—that is all I wish, for now."

"But, once Areel is out of the way, those two will still continue to terrorize Shadizar," said Sonja.

"I don't care about what happens to Shadizar!" Sendes shook his head impatiently, angrily. "Areel is a dangerous witch—she must be destroyed. Once I've accomplished that, I'm sure Nalor will be convinced of my loyalty, and then I'll be able to go about as I please once more, without the threat of death breathing down my neck."

Sonja felt a sudden disgust for the young Corinthian.

"Which means you must confront your angry lord, and Kus, after confronting Areel and her sorcery. Have you really got the courage for all that, Sendes?"

Sendes shook his head tolerantly. "I have no choice. If I can slay Areel—if I can take her head to Nalor—he will forgive me, and I can then do as I please."

"Somehow, I can't quite picture Nalor letting by-gones be bygones. But—" the Hyrkanian shrugged. "Now, as to Areel—do you and Lera have a plan?"

"Aye." Sendes regarded Sonja questioningly.

"I won't interfere," she told him. "And if I can help, you may be able to provoke some of my good nature to the surface—even if you can't pay me in gold."

"This is between Areel and me," said Sendes. "I have it all planned. Here, Lera." He produced a piece of parchment from his tunic and handed it to the girl.

Lera regarded it for a moment; a diagram of lines with a hastily written note signed by Nalor. "This can't be real," she said to Sendes. "How did you come by it?"

He frowned a smile. "I drew it up myself, that's how."

"What do you intend to do with it?"

"Go on—read it. It's a note from Nalor to Kus, outlining a plan to slay Areel and bury her in the grove where you and I met. It is dated for tonight; Kus is to capture Areel and bring her to the grove, where he and Nalor will sacrifice her to the dark gods."

Slowly Lera shook her head. "They would never—"

"They might. In any case, Areel doesn't know them well enough to know *what* they might do, especially this far along in the game—as Sonja chooses to call it."

"And what am I to do with this?" asked Lera.

"Show it to Areel. Tell her you found it last night, after Kus broke in, and let her read it. The discrepancy in dates will only serve to convince her; she will expect Kus to arrive again tonight. If I know her, she will head for the grove at midnight, expecting to find Nalor there alone and kill him. Then she will wait for Kus, hoping to destroy him also. But she won't find Nalor, or Kus. She won't find anything but my sword, waiting to hack off her head."

Silence, for a long moment.

"And you think this will work?" Sonja asked.

"It will work," Sendes snapped back, "because I know Areel. I know how impetuous she is; she thinks so much of herself that she supposes everything will go the way she wants it to. It will work."

Sonja grunted, shifted in her chair and felt the talisman within her pouch. She had mentioned it, but not shown it; Sendes had not asked to see it, and now—wrapped up in his own scheme—he did not suppose that it might be of any use to him.

She stood up, stretched, made to leave.

Sendes said: "Remember, you've promised not to interfere with us, Sonja."

"And why should I interfere? To save your neck, Sendes? My only worry is that, even should you slay Areel, Nalor and Kus will still be around to cause trouble. No—no—I won't interfere. I just hope you're as quick with your sword as you seem to be with your wits."

She spent the rest of the day looking for work, and trying to get things out of her mind and convince herself that, while it had been a fluke that she had become involved in these episodes at all, her involvement was now over.

Late in the afternoon she signed up with a nobleman's caravan; it was heading west on a buying trip through Corinthia, Ophir and Numdia, leaving in a week and returning in two months. The nobleman wanted bodyguards and escorts; his chief officer promised Sonja wages equal to that given to any male soldiers serving, in return for equal service. Sonja affixed her name in ink to the registration for employment, then winked to the nobleman's officer as she exited.

She ate at a small tavern, downed two tankards of ale

and tried to clear her thoughts while watching the men in the place make asses of themselves over the girls dancing in the corner. Walking home in the rain, she tried to convince herself not to do anything outlandish—such as trailing Sendes to the grove outside the city tonight, to save his butt from Areel's sorcery. Sendes might think he knew Areel, but Sonja knew sorcery—and she had tasted Areel's sorcery. Never, in all her strange career, had she grown used to the flavor of evil that sorcery brings to things; but knowing that flavor kept her aware, on guard and resilient, whereas others who knew nothing about it might blunder in and get their skins burned. She thought back to the fete Nalor had given, and Sendes' casual dismissal of Sonja's charge that Kus performed true sorcery. A perfect example!

Outside her apartment she bought some cheese and fruit from a vendor. As expected, she found Chost still asleep in her room. Surely he must have needed his rest, poor kid—half-starved as he was and living constantly on the energy of fear awakened by the uncertain life of the streets. Life in jungles and wild forests was safer than trying to make one's way, defenseless, in the jungles and forests of civilization—and Sonja, regarded by some as a barbarian, knew the hard truth of this.

She placed the food on a table, sank down on her bed and stretched out her legs. The disturbance made Chost roll over beside her, but he did not awaken. Sonja studied the boy in the dull light of the rainy day. Not really a boy, not yet a man—perhaps Lera's age. Young in years, old in experience. . . . Sonja pondered it. When she was this boy's age, she had still been virginal in her awareness of the world. It had only been later, too short a time later, that she had learned so violently and painfully what a hell earth is, how ironically and insanely it rocks between the touchstones of joy and ecstasy on the one side, agony and horror on the other. It was a wonder she could never fathom: how the good, kindly people she occasionally met could survive in such a monstrous world—or, how such evil and carnage and destruction as she had known could continue if the good gods proposed by the pious truly existed. The whole world rocked, swayed, jumbled itself uncertainly.

"It is a web," someone had told her once, "—a web, with everything in it commingled, and the gods know the plan, but we just blunder through."

Blunder through—that described her life fairly well. Sometimes the joy she felt, travelling alone in a woods, or sitting before a fire someplace with good companions, seemed all out of proportion to what she should experience as a spirit emplaced in frail human flesh. At other times, life seemed so weary, so depressing and maddening—so pointless and frustrating and unhumorous in its black jokes—that the suicide cult of the Mariiks seemed to have a sensible argument going for them.

But what often astonished Sonja above all else was the indomitable will of most people: not just the warriors, who vainly paraded their glory and strength, nor the merchants, the nobles, the chieftains and power-mongers, but the ordinary people without titles, power or money. History for most was a list of king's names, battles, patriarchs or religious ideas. But history for the little people of the world, the common men and women, was a list of ancestors, of work accomplished, of quiet devotions, of ale and laughter, griefs and tears, births and burials, memories and dreams. Theirs were small ambitions made great by the uncomplicated lives of those who achieved them—without fanfare, without money, without broadsheets tacked to walls or temple bells extolling the news. The ordinary people of the earth—the people of the cities and the farms—lived their lives, squabbled, prayed to their gods, shared their bread and cheese and water, offered comfort to strangers, and lived their lives of quiet accomplishment. Without influence, power did not corrupt them; without wealth, money could not make them mad; without high ambition luring them on to war, they kept to their simple gods of hearth and home, childbirth and gaming. And because of these people, so taken for granted, so maligned by those with greater wealth and power—only because of them, Sonja reflected, could those with greater advantage have any advantage at all. If all men had equal wealth, who might lord it over them? If all men had an equal voice, then who with one voice might drown out their common humanity?

Yet it never had been that way, and never would be. The common folk, always and always, would bear on their backs, silently, the long succession of barons and dukes and kings, money-men and power-men; and while those men built temples in their own names and created wars for their own glory, the common people, nameless, would go on creating new lives, creating the true foundation of it all, without fanfare, without broadsheets, without temple bells.

Once, in some village she couldn't name now, Sonja had sat with an old woman, and together they had watched two young scamps wrestling in the dust.

"There it is," the old woman had said. "Our future—the meaning of life. Our sons and daughters. That is what life is for; that is why Nature, through the gods, made us. To continue. For, continuing, we try.

With each new life, we try to better ourselves. I will not live to see it—they may not live to see it—but someday? Their children, or their children's children, may live to see it. Do you recall your religion? Once earth was paradise; the gods created earth and all things on it according to their will. But when humans rebelled, the gods filled them with all the vices and told them that when the day came that they had cast out those vices, men would again be in paradise. So that is why we live. For the children. To teach them. Some may stray, some may learn. Different ideas all come from the same mind, from the mind of the gods; we must learn to winnow, that is all. We continue to live so that we may have children. For their sake, the gods made the world. For their sake—not ours."

For their sake. Yet, every human began as a child—and in the end, age and death took them all. Sonja had been touched by the old woman, but had been unable to believe. She seemed to feel the old woman's desperate need for a meaning in life—but was that meaning really there?

Sonja looked down at Chost, so young yet so aged in some ways, and wondered briefly at the woman she was. For she *was* a woman. A woman in armor, a woman with a sword—true—but also a woman with virtues and vices, living with secret hopes and ambitions, some coming true, some not—a woman who bled every month, like all those women she saw on the streets. And yet, a woman without children—without that promise for the future.

She looked at Chost and wondered if, in some other world, some other history, some other life—if, somehow, in some other way, she might have been granted a son like Chost. If life had gone differently—if lives were truly reincarnated.

She steeled herself against the thoughts. There was no sense to it. She rose off the bed, went to the table, sliced herself some cheese.

Chost awoke, sat up and rubbed his eyes. "Sonja?"

"Aye, I'm here."

"What hour is it? Gods! Have I slept the whole day?"

"Aye," Sonja told him. "You slept the whole day. You must have been having pleasant dreams, Chost. Very pleasant dreams. . . ."

Areel studied the letter, studied Lera's frightened face, then looked again to the letter.

"Why did you not tell me of this earlier?"

"I—I was too frightened to read it until today, mistress."

"Indeed." Areel fingered the parchment, studied the script. "It appears to be in Nalor's hand, all right. This may be my opportunity. How fortunate. The fools!"

Lera breathed somewhat more easily.

"So . . . tonight, is it?" She walked to an oil lamp, fed the parchment to the flames. "Tonight, then. I shall be there—and they shall face avenging sorcery, and a woman's wrath."

Lera turned to go.

"You will come with me, Lera."

"Mistress?"

"I may have need of you. You will come with me."

"Y-yes, mistress."

"Go, now."

"Yes, mistress. . . ."

The door closed softly.

"Aye," Areel muttered; "If I have need of you. And, if I have need to sacrifice a virgin's soul to the hell-demons, I *will* have need of you. . . ."

Chapter 8.

Evening—and still the rain fell outside. Nalor found himself idly wondering if this would be the beginning of the Flood which prophets said would drown the world.

The last glimmer of daylight had disappeared long ago. Nalor knew, however, that despite the clouds which hid the sunset, Kus would not arrive until the sun had fully disappeared beyond the rim of the earth, away into the chasm of night. He ordered his meal and ate it alone.

Kus arrived silently half-way through the meal, and sat opposite Nalor. The Councillor regarded him scrupulously.

"Are you not supping? Drinking?"

Kus' eyes flashed darkly. "Who was that red-haired woman who defied me at your fete some nights ago, Nalor?"

"I have no idea."

"Her name is Red Sonja, and she used to live in a rooming house in the southern section of the city, between the main boulevard and the Street of the Wine-merchants. So much I learned by divination and inquiry. But now she has changed quarters, and some magic seems to protect her from my divinations. I should like to find her."

"Shouldn't you be thinking of finding Areel, instead?"

Kus showed a white grin. "She may even be aiding Areel," he said in his serpent's hiss. "The woman is no witch, and yet there is now some sort of sorcery protecting her. Finding her may lead us to finding Areel. Besides, I want her for myself. I will not slay her; I will merely—initiate her into the ranks of the *ilorku*. You truly do not know where she is?"

"At some cheap apartment, I presume. Or, perhaps she has left Shadizar altogether."

"No." Kus rose. "She remains in Shadizar, and I will find her." He chortled grotesquely. "I had a harem once—twenty lovely beauties, each initiated into the dark lessons of Ordru, each a lunatic for the taste of life's scarlet wine, each wholly and utterly deceptive in allurement and intelligence. But they were stolen from me."

"Stolen from you?"

"It was a long, long time ago, Nalor. They were stolen from me—slain. Ohh, yes, we can be destroyed. It is true. But such as you do not know how, nor will you ever."

Nalor winced. "I know some things, Kus. Sunlight, certain sorcerous rituals can—"

"But I control you, Nalor," Kus whispered. "I know you. I *own* you. You bargained yourself to me months ago, by participating in the rites of Semrog. You have no power over me whatsoever." He turned on his heel, went to the door, pivoted again. "Creature of the day," he said slowly, "what a phantom you are! You and your kind are children to me, children who age and wither and die, having learned nothing—no wisdom, no insight. You fear death, you malign and misuse life. Fools! You pass like rain, Nalor—you come and are gone, you and yours. . . . While I and my kind, alive in graves and coffins, hidden in shadows, conversing with demons, fired by Hell's own flame and with the sigil of our immortal caste in our veins—we laugh at you, and devour you, and raise a few of you to our own level. . . ."

With that, he was gone—swiftly, silently, like a shadow.

Nalor sat alone, hands trembling as he tried to spoon his cold soup—soup gone cold in the icy presence of Kus.

Nalor, alone, with the evening darkness and the rain and the cold—

Wondering how he might, indeed, destroy Kus.

The rain began to let up, though the wind continued to moan out across the field-lands beyond the gate. To Sendes' ears came the quiet, murmuring trickle of water seeping into the earth and the endless drip-drip-dripping of raindrops rolling down broad leaves and striking the ground, the bushes, the rocks, the fallen logs.

The city wall, looming high through the whispering wet trees, glowed with torchlight. Shadows of troops intermittently lined the parapets, on their nightly patrol. Other than that, there was only the silence of the night, and clouds moving like gray phantoms, against the full moon's broad face. The silence—

Broken.

Footsteps—more than of one person—sounded on the brick and cobbled pathway leading from the gate. Sendes pulled himself erect, dug the fingers of one hand into tree bark for support, tightened his other hand around his sword-hilt. Droplets fell upon his blond hair and he shook them away. A damp chill seeped down his spine; he curled his toes inside his boots.

Two figures, yes—robed in gray, fluttering through the misty night. Two women. They came closer down the pathway, approaching the spot where Sendes waited—

Waited, with sword bared, glistening with rain.

He breathed deeply, aware that he had been holding his breath, and never did the fragrance of a freshly-awakened forest vivify his senses as did this grove, to-night, as he stood waiting to deal death to a sorceress who had betrayed him.

The footsteps sounded closer. The wind moaned. Sendes could see their faces in the gray moonlight.

She had fallen asleep! Damn Mitra, damn all the gods for allowing her to fall asleep! Had she been that tired? She had not exerted herself especially. . . .

Sonja quickened her pace. The northwestern gate was yet far away, far away, and the bells of Shadizar were tolling the midnight hour with deep, thundering peals.

Damn the gods for letting her fall asleep!

She had had only a glass of wine, then returned to her room to see if Chost, by chance, were there. He was not. To rest her legs, she had sat on the bed, then had lain back, fully awake. . . .

And had awakened suddenly, only moments ago, as if from a dream. There had been no nightmare, no strange phantoms. And yet—

Sonja was still tired—woozy—and not from wine. It was almost as if something had made her fall asleep. Something in her wine? Something sent by Areel, or Kus?

She ran faster, her boots splashing in rain puddles, her sword clacking at her side—across streets, around corners, through alleys.

Damn the gods! And damn Sendes for being a young fool!

* * *

"Girl," said Areel, listening to the wind, "I sense no sorcery here. Yet, something is amiss—"

"Areel!"

She turned, eyes glowing yellow in the dark, robe flowing out slowly like a net of shadow to capture damp moonlight.

Sendes was a voice and a sudden movement; only his face, blurred gray, showed from the shadows for a moment—and his sword, streaking silvery in the darkness of the thick foliage.

Lera screamed and jumped back. "Sendes!" she cried involuntarily.

Areel hissed; Sendes leaped at her, his sword up.

"Witch! For betraying me!"

Somehow, with supple ease, Areel avoided the fierce blow. Whirling, she threw out her arm toward the Corinthian and yelled some words in an unknown tongue. Instantly her stiffened hand glowed eerily, as if white-hot. Then, as Sendes' sword began another savage arc, she jerked her arm—

And Sendes screamed.

Lera, having fallen to the ground in her terror, threw a hand to her mouth and drew up her legs, trying to back away, not believing despite all she had come to believe.

Sendes' scream was cut short as though by a sudden paroxysm. Areel hissed venomously as the bolt of white light streamed from her fist into the Corinthian's chest. The sword, masterless, leapt through the air and slid away on the damp grass.

Sendes fell on his side, rolled onto his back, feet twitching, eyes wide. The dew dampened one side of his face. One hand, clawed with pain, ripped at his tunic over his chest; the other, shuddering, gripped the wet grass and pulled furrows in the mud.

He croaked: "Godsss. . . !"

Then his head fell back—in death.

Areel turned to Lera. "You! You knew all along! Wench! Little bitch! What were you trying to do?"

Lera's scream carried to the moon as she tried to back away, pushing with her legs, hips writhing in the grass.

Through the gate Sonja came, running, the damp air of midnight in her lungs—away from the dim city lights, nearly stumbling on the uneven stones and bricks of the pathway.

The grove, just ahead. Sonja ran faster, heart pumping, legs nearly numb, hair floating and flopping around her ears, eyes aching, sweat trickling under her mail shirt—

There! Two figures in robes, one on the ground—but where was Sendes? Mitra and Hotath! Had she slain him already?

Still running, Sonja jerked free her blade; it rasped from its sheath like the bared fang of a dragon. In the same instant a girl's scream rang to the skies.

"Areel!" yelled Sonja.

The witch turned, tall in the moonlight, shadowy gray against the black backdrop of trees and shrubbery. Lera lay on the ground, screaming.

"You!" Areel shrieked, lifting her arm.

Sonja instinctively threw herself to one side as Areel's arm glowed. Something like a beam of power barely missed her. With her free hand she yanked the talisman from her belt-pouch, slackened her pace, lifted the object. . . .

It glowed like a white coal in the moonlight, throwing a light upon Areel's face, breast, arms—

Areel hissed, held up her hands, backed away.

160

"Get up, girl!" cried Sonja, running to Lera. "On your feet!" She stood by the girl as she lay gasping for breath, trying to rise. Her own breath came in gasps as she confronted the witch, sword shivering in her right hand, talisman glowing in her upheld left—

Still glowing, lighting Areel's beautiful features with its glow.

"Give that—to me!" snarled Areel, her witch's eyes burning like yellow diamonds.

"Lera—behind me! Quickly!"

"It's mine—mine!" screamed Areel. Evidently she could not stand the talisman's glow, for she fell back another step, and another, away from the light. Her legs trembled.

"Walk backwards, Lera. Hurry! Get away from here! I'll follow!"

Areel half-tripped; she crumpled to the ground, shielding her eyes.

"It pains you?" Sonja asked the witch tensely. But she did not wait for a reply, for if the guards on the wall had heard anything, a patrol might be heading for them even now. "Witch, remember who has it! Remember what I can do with it!" She turned briefly to Lera. "Run, girl!"

Then she backed away herself, down the path— walking backwards, leaving Areel cringing on the wet grass, a few paces from Sendes' blasted corpse.

Lera sobbed, "Sonja, I—"

"Quiet, just keep going!"

Areel's form was absorbed into the darkness as the talisman's light receded from her, till only the twin coals of her eyes were visible, gleaming yellowly. Then those eyes vanished as if they had blinked shut, and Sonja guessed the witch had fled among the trees, a shadow swallowed by the greater shadow of night.

Finally, when they were near the gate—when the grove was but a distant clump of darkness—Sonja turned and dropped the talisman into her pouch and sheathed her sword, then grabbed Lera by the arm. "Now, come on—quickly! To my apartment! She'll try to follow, and I don't know how much time we have!"

Chost and five of his friends had helped themselves to Sonja's apartment, a little after midnight, by climbing in through the window. There was food on a table—wine, cheese, bread and some fine morsels of crisp, honeyed dough—so Chost and Stiva and the four others helped themselves.

They did not light a lamp. While they were eating, they decided they would wait up till Sonja returned, just to make sure she knew who'd been there. Finishing their meal, they sat in a circle on the floor before the window, and in the pale moonlight began to recount their various adventures of the day. One of them had to use the chamber-pot, and so tinkled away while the others made ribald comments.

The moonlight disappeared from the window as he rejoined his friends, but none of them commented on it.

Two yawned.

Chost said, "Strange, how sleepy I feel. . . ."

The moonlight did not return. Chost thought he detected a black mist at the window, smoking up, filling the panes, spilling into the room and coalescing an arm's length from his companions—but the sight evoked only an idle curiosity in him.

The boys were falling asleep—not so strange, Chost thought, considering their weariness—leaning against one another, stretching out on the floor, sinking into abysses of dream. . . .

The smoke hissed. Yellow eyes gleamed from the black mist and a hand began to form, tightening, muscling, becoming real. And Chost, strangely unalarmed, felt himself drifting into soothing visions of heavy, honey-flavored slumber.

Sonja suspected nothing as she and Lera mounted the steps to her apartment; she smelled no strange scents, heard no cries, sensed no peril.

She opened the door of her room, still uneasily reliving her encounter with Areel and wondering what would happen tomorrow—and saw Kus standing tall and dark before the open window, backlit with moonlight, holding a young boy in his arms. The lad's head was tilted back at an unnatural angle; his eyes were open and glazed with death; blood drooled in loose drops from his throat to the floor. Kus, looking up, glared with yellow eyes that stopped Sonja in her tracks.

"Erlik!" she gasped.

Kus hissed, and a spray of blood formed a filmy curtain for an instant before his face. He dropped his young victim to the floor; the corpse, drained to stiff whiteness, landed with an inhuman thud, and the sound did not awaken the lad's companions.

It suddenly seemed to Sonja that Kus—black, shadowed, evil, glowing with the incandescence of the lightless flames of Hell—grew many feet taller, towered over her, and that the room shrank. Her heart and instincts, for one moment, also shrank—withered—died.

The vampire's eyes were stealing her from herself. . . .

Then Sonja's animal instincts awakened. With a surge of desperation she averted her eyes from Kus.

"Lera! Away!" She backed up, threw out an arm,

struck the girl on the cheek. Lera staggered back into the hallway, fell against a wall, crumpled soundlessly to the floor—

And Sonja jumped in, kicked the door closed and drew her sword.

"Vampire!"

Kus hissed, grinning horribly.

"Ilorku!"

Red slobber drooled down the sorcerer's pale chin. "You," he growled. "It is you—I want!"

Sonja, watching him narrowly, sensing that he could move with the rapidity of a phantom, yelled to the boys: "Chost! All of you! Wake up! *Wake up!*"

"They cannot awaken," Kus laughed, "unless I so command them. They dream my dreams, and soon they will sleep my sleep."

"Monster—!"

"I know you, Red Sonja of Hyrkania!" Kus gurgled, the blood still in his throat. "You have fought sorcery and demons aforetime, and now you dare to fight me. You sought to protect yourself with witchcraft—I can feel it upon you even now. Did you cast some feeble spell, Red Witch, thinking you could evade me? Ha-ha-ha! Your magic hid you briefly, and even warded off the vampire-sleep I sent forth when I found you earlier this night—but now you are mine. You shall fight sorcery no longer, for sorcery has overcome you; you shall slay no more demons, for now you shall yourself become one! You shall hunger for the blood, hide from the daylight, slumber in coffins and perform the rites to Semrog and Ordru. Fall to your knees!"

Sonja raised her sword—and instantly it felt heavier than a mountain in her hand. Kus' eyes glared, and Sonja felt yellow flames bursting within her brain, dancing behind her eyes, commanding her. The immense weight of her sword pulled her down.

She dropped to her knees.

"Crawl!" Kus commanded, baring his teeth with great glee. "Crawl! Crawl to me and beg for my hungry kiss. *Crawllll! Red Sonja!*"

She wavered. She dropped her sword. Her head floated to the right, to the left, backwards, forward —floating. . . . Cascading music filled her mind. Visions of childhood engulfed her—visions of her mother and father, their security—and she saw it all returned to Kus, who promised her the sweet repose of childhood, wonderful moonlight and warm earth, unending dreams and scarlet rivers to slake her thirst. . . .

She crawled. Her bare knees scraped on the wooden floor, bumped against Chost and his companions. Sonja crawled over them, staring up at Kus, whose height continued to grow, whose yellow eyes continued to burn and beckon like two torches leading her homeward from the depths of a lonely forest.

Home . . . Kus. . . .

"Come, Sonja, yes . . . come. . . ."

Yet even as her skin flushed, as her arms grew weighted and her brain danced with visions, she felt an instinct—a growl in her soul—something deep, primordial and human from a time when humans were their true barbaric selves—a whisper that denied Kus. . . .

"Come, Sonja. . . ."

A voice, that denied Kus. . . .

"Yes . . . come, Sonja. Crawl. . . ."

A mental scream, a savage release that denied Kus. . . .

"Yes, yes, come, now I will reward you. . . ."

No!

"I am here." He bent over her. "You love me, Sonja." His yellow eyes washed their light down over her face. "I am everything, Sonja."

His rank breath blasted her cheek.

"No-oho-ohhh!"

Her desperation, her horror, her scream born of primordial fear, pushed her back. Kus laughed and reached for her—

And Sonja, seeing herself as in a dream, drove both hands into her belt-pouch, withdrew the talisman—

Kus' eyes whitened.

Sonja struggled to rise, to stand up. She rocked on trembling feet—and Kus backed away. She threw up her hands, the talisman glowing whitely in them—and Kus screamed.

Sonja threw herself forward with all her dimming strength. The talisman struck Kus full on the chest. The white glow seemed to fill him; a white smoke blew up and there was a burning, hissing sound. Kus shrieked and threw himself back.

Then black mist filled the room, clouding the window. The vampire was changing form, dissolving, retreating. Sonja fell forward, clinging to the talisman as if to her soul, her life.

She saw an apparition at the panes—black fog that screamed in an unearthly, soundless wail as it withdrew across the sill like a roiling carpet.

She slumped to the floor, clutching the talisman beneath her, falling on it as her face and knees and elbows struck on the rough planking.

She dreamed of coffins that screamed in the sunlight. . . .

She awoke, realizing that only a short time could have passed. Most of the feeling of horror was gone; the evil had withdrawn in retreat. Dimly she heard a woman sobbing, and rolled over.

Was it the first light of dawn filtering through the window, or did the talisman still glow whitely as she clutched it in her hands?

Lera, crouching beside the bed, was sobbing and crying, hands to her face, shoulders shuddering, hair tumbled.

Sonja fell back to sleep with the white light in her brain, utter fatigue in her limbs and the smell of curdled blood in her nostrils.

Areel had made it safely home to her apartment—not through the northwestern gate of Shadizar, for even as her strength quickly returned she had heard city guards coming down the path to investigate the screams from the grove.

While the moon rose higher she had travelled outside the city walls, hugging close to the shadows, breathing in the cool night air, which helped to revivify her. Finally she had re-entered the city through another small gate in the north wall, and returned by the alleyways and back streets to her apartment.

In her chamber, she lit oil lamps, then fell exhausted into a chair, staring at herself in a mirror. In the lamplight her eyes and trembling lips seemed unusually dark against the pallor of her drawn face.

So Red Sonja the Hyrkanian had the talisman, and knew that it was a weapon against sorcery!

Areel cursed at the thought. She must gain the talisman herself, for whoever owned it, owned its power. If she could come by it, she could destroy Nalor and Kus. She could—

But she did not own the talisman.

She must get it. She must get to Red Sonja—must. . . .

Then she was asleep and dreaming deeply, lips murmuring of what she must do, before she had become aware of just how exhausted she was.

* *

It was mid-morning, and Sonja was awake, aware and burning with anger. Lera and the boys stood silently, ashen-faced—save for Stiva, Chost's friend, who lay dead upon the floor.

Sonja gave Lera money. "Take Chost and the other boys out of here," she told her. "Take them somewhere and buy yourselves some food. And stay away until I come for you."

They went—shaking, nervous and uncertain.

Sonja waited until they had gone, then covered Stiva's body with a blanket from her bed and went out, walked to an office of the city patrol three streets over and reported the crime.

Somewhat to her surprise, they did not eye her with suspicion or ask leading questions. There had been another strange murder last night, in a grove outside the walls. Shadizar was full of crime. The death of a small, blood-drained boy was doubtless the work of the same mad killer who had committed several such deeds already, and who seemed to elude capture as easily as though he faded into thin air afterwards.

"Who was the boy? Son? Brother? Cousin?"

"His name was Stiva. No relation. I'm passing through town; he was a street urchin, begging. I took him in to give him food and rest. He fell asleep. I went out, got back late—and found him dead. Drained of blood."

One of the officials commented: "Now he's breaking into places, this throat-tearer. Usually he hangs around alleys and behind taverns."

Sonja looked at him. "Have you any idea who he might be?"

The official shrugged. "We're offering no opinions just yet, and we'd advise against idle talk. The city's reputation—"

"I find it hard to believe that Shadizar's reputation

could sink lower than it already is," Sonja interrupted.

"Still, we're a caravan-center, and we would hate to have any trade scared off. You know how it is—"

"But with an *ilorku* killer loose—"

"Don't use that word, please," said the official sternly.

"*Ilorku*? Why not?"

"There's panic already in the streets, and displeasure in high places. I don't believe in vampires, myself, but we can't have idle gossip. Just makes things worse."

"Aye," echoed a second official. "We can't have gossip."

Sonja frowned. "You're going to have more than gossip on your hands if you don't catch this maniac."

With that, she left. After taking her breakfast in a small tavern, she returned to her room in time to find city officials carrying out Stiva's body—and in time for her landlord to take her aside and ask her just why the hell the killer had picked *her* room and *his* apartment house for his latest outrage. Bad for business. Sonja realized that she wasn't scoring any points in *this* game of knife throw.

"You want me to leave? Is that it?"

The landlord's fat face scowled. "I'm just going to keep an eye on you."

"I'll leave, damn it, just say so. Better than having you carrying on so churlishly."

"I'm just going to keep my one good eye on you, outlander. And remember, it's a sharp eye. Woman with a sword! Pfeh!"

She went looking for Lera and Chost, and soon found them. The other young scamps had taken off for alleys unknown, but Lera and Chost were sitting on a bench in a nearby square, finishing their bread and talking in low voices. Sonja sat beside them.

"They've taken Stiva. I'm sorry, Chost."

The lad said nothing; his face showed no emotion.

"I know who did it," Sonja went on. "The officials don't, and couldn't act if they did. But I can."

"Who was it?" Chost's voice was hushed, strained.

"If I tell you, you'll get a gang together thinking you can settle it yourselves. And if you do, you'll all get killed."

"No, we won't."

"Don't even think of it, Chost. I'm used to trouble, but last night was nearly too much trouble for me to handle. We're alive only because I was lucky enough to have the right weapon. But I'm really beginning to put some pieces together now. Lera, are you all right?"

She nodded briskly, showing more enthusiasm than she felt. "It was Kus, wasn't it, Sonja?"

Sonja sighed. "Aye."

"He came into my mistress' house in the same way, the night he slew the guards. Areel, too, has some magical amulets; she says they saved my life, but I don't know. I felt Kus might have killed me had he cared to. . . ."

"What're we going to do about it?" Chost asked.

"*I'm* going to kill the monster," Sonja replied. "I know how, and I've got the thing that'll do it. You don't, Chost."

The boy stared at the ground in silence.

"Chost?"

"Did I say anything?"

"I know what you're thinking," said Sonja. "Tarim's blood! If you want to go and wind up like your friend Stiva—"

She stopped speaking as she saw his pained look.

"Sorry." Sonja tousled his hair, looked away gravely, studied the square. The city was coming to life around them. "Come on."

She stood up and led the way back toward her apartment. Chost and Lera followed, holding hands as they did so. Sonja glanced back and saw them.

Wonderful, she thought. Splendid. Why don't you two youngsters just fall in love and complicate matters even more. . . ?

Chapter 9.

Nalor finished his breakfast, but the food did not settle the anxious thrill that played in his stomach. He wiped his lips, rose up and paced his room, thoughtful. He strode to the window and looked out at the sunlight that played upon the trees and grass and brick-cobbled walk-ways.

A man-servant crossed the room and began cleaning up the dishes and trays. "My lord, shall I announce that you will be in your audience hall momentarily?"

"What?" He turned from the window. "No, no, not yet. Hold up on that a moment. Is business pressing?"

"There are men from the city guard here—I believe they are concerned about the rash of murders in the city. Also, the usual envoys from the palace, and a few merchants. . . ."

"Let them wait. Take the dishes and be gone."

"As my lord wishes."

When the man had exited, Nalor walked to a weapon-rack across the chamber, undid its latch and opened the panel. Ranks of blades gleamed—swords, knives, spears, short-swords, daggers. It was one of his hobbies to collect strange and antique weapons. He reached up, took down an old knife of Stygian make which someone had told him was exceedingly old. It was an intriguing weapon because it was not made of bronze, as were most Stygian weapons of the period, but of iron. Because it showed relatively little wear, despite its great age, Nalor and some associates had concluded that it had probably served as a ritual knife of some kind—or perhaps had never been used at all, save as an ornament.

Or perhaps, a scholarly judge had told Nalor one night over wine, it had been meant to slay *ilorkim* which, legend said, had been rife in Stygia a millenium ago.

Nalor grinned nervously, hefted the knife in his hand.

It was not the only iron knife in that rack; and in every other weapon-rack, in every other chamber of his apartment, Nalor likewise had placed similar iron weapons. He had never intended to use them against vampires; but more than once, after Kus had made his appearance, Nalor had more than idly reflected on those weapons.

He closed the rack, locked it, shoved the iron knife into his belt, then left his chamber via a small door and went down a narrow stairwell. The steps were hidden within an interior passage in the old building. When Nalor had first purchased the place and learned of these secret passageways, he had ordered the doors locked; now only he used them, to spy upon guests, or to make his way unseen from one place to another within his home.

Now he followed the stairwells to their bottom, to the old earth cellars and catacombs beneath the house—to where Kus, in this lightless den of holes and gravel and ancient stone, homed during the deadly daylight hours.

The stone sarcophagus was in one of the farthest chambers of the cellars. Nalor knew the way, though he had not traversed it often. Only twice had he come down here in the months since Kus had arrived: the first time, to show the vampire where he might hide during the daylight, the second time with his guards chasing down a house-servant who had sought to escape a punishment. It had been just after sunset, and half-way down the stairs they had heard screams, then dark laughter, then more screams—and pursued no more. Neither did Kus make an appearance that night.

Nalor took down a torch from the wall. It was cold and nearly fresh. He struck sparks with flint and a steel rasp; the gummy tar of the torch-end caught quickly, sending up thick rings of black smoke. Holding the torch ahead of him, Nalor walked several steps, then decided that the center chamber—yes—was where Kus lay hidden.

The torchlight was a glowing ball in the center of the room, sending Nalor's shadow rippling upon cracked flags and chipped brick. Rats scurried out of the way, re-hid themselves in dirty niches in far corners. Cobwebs brushed Nalor's face; he gasped and brushed them away.

Cobwebs?

A thought struck him: Should not the cobwebs have been brushed away by Kus, every night, as he made his exit from this hole. . . ?

Half-way across the stagnant chamber, the torch-light—wavering in Nalor's nervous grip—showed the ancient stone sarcophagus resting upon an altar of basalt. Whoever had been put to final rest in it had been done away with long ago—probably looters had stolen the body hoping to find jewelry under the wrappings—before apartments had been built over the tunnels, perhaps even before Shadizar had been more than a crossroads trading center. Did this chamber date all the way back to Acheron? Was there yet air in here that had been breathed by those who had buried their dead in that age?

Nalor was sweating, though he shivered with fear. Was Kus sending him unsettling thoughts from within that stone coffin?

There was a sconce on the wall; Nalor rested his torch in it, drew his knife from his belt and approached the stone sarcophagus. Its lid sat as high as his chest.

Mitra, he thought—*Mitra, guide me in this deed.*

With cold fingers he pushed up on the lid of the sarcophagus. It was very heavy. He pried with the knife; the lid loosened with an audible sound, a hiss. Dust or mist seemed to escape for a moment, blowing up into the Lord Councillor's face. Nalor coughed.

But the lid was loosened.

With the heels of his hands he shoved against the stone lid. It slid awkwardly, turning at an angle so that the inside was partly visible. Nalor looked down into the coffin.

Kus appeared as a sleeping corpse. There was no sign of breathing, no flicker of the closed eyelids, no sign of life whatsoever—though Nalor knew very well that if he did not plunge his knife into the monster's breast, Kus would awaken at twilight and climb up the stone stairwell, come into his study—

Mitra, aid me! Gods, guide my hand!

He procrastinated no more, but raised the iron knife, aimed its point for Kus' chest—

Then, incredibly, though there was no sound or sign of movement, it was as though Nalor's mind had blanked out for a moment. In the next moment he awoke. His hand was still raised; the dagger had not plunged—

And Kus' eyes were open and alive—terribly alive, flaming with yellow light—and his hand was gripping Nalor's wrist, the wrist of the hand that rested, shuddering, on the edge of the sarcophagus.

Fool! Worm! Did you think I would not see and know, though I lie here in my silent sleep? Did you forget the power I hold over you because of your participation in the rites of Semrog?

"Mitra—aid me—!" Nalor breathed hoarsely.

Mitra does not exist, O man of flesh. I exist only, and you.

"Oh, godsss—!"

There are no gods.

"No-ohh!" Nalor shrieked, hauling back his arm, dropping the knife. It clattered on the floor behind him, in the dimness—but Kus' eyes still glowed, and his clutch did not release Nalor.

Be warned! When I awake, I will come for you. Fool! Fool!

The glow of the eyes dimmed; Kus' hand released its grip.

Nalor, gasping, threw himself backward from Kus' hold, staggered into the darkness, almost fell.

As if alive, or by a will of its own, the stone lid of the sarcophagus slid back, covering up Kus.

Breathing hoarsely, screams strangling in his throat, Nalor turned and ran. Stumbling down the corridor, he caught hold of the wall and threw himself up the stairs, ran and ran, still hearing Kus' terrible, soundless voice in his mind. . . .

It was not easy for Areel to swallow her pride and decide at last to go to Sonja and argue that, despite all that had occurred, the two of them were essentially on the same side—against Nalor, and against Kus. But the fact was irrefutable, the necessity unequivocal. So by mid-morning, after rising and bathing herself, Areel had dressed in a crimson robe, strung many ornaments and jewelries upon her arms, waist and throat, and had exited her apartment.

She took a street carriage to the apartment, and experienced a touch of nausea—not sickness, merely her struggling pride—as she entered by the alley door. A wave of recollection came over her for a moment: the old feeling she had suffered in coming here earlier, to visit Osumu. Forcing the feeling down, she closed the door behind her, walked down the hall to the room where she sensed Sonja resided. The emotions were powerful.

For a moment she stood in the hallway, outside that door. It was marked by a crimson dragon. How fitting, Areel thought. The amulet she sought symbolized something like a dragon. Then she heard voices from within—one unmistakably Sonja's, and two others— and rapped on the wood.

Almost immediately the door opened. Red Sonja, the Hyrkanian warrior-woman, stood there in her shirt of mail, her flamelike hair cascading down her shoulders and back, sapphire eyes blazing with vitality. The longsword on her left hip and the links of her mail glowed with a dull sheen.

Their eyes met instantly, and held.

If Sonja were surprised, she concealed it well, only scowling slightly and whispering in a chilly tone: "Well, damn me to the Hells, 'tis a demon in Areel's form."

Behind her, Lera and a street urchin stood up from the edge of the bed, held their places and stared. Areel marked them well.

"No demon, Hyrkanian," she responded in as cold a tone. "No, it is I, myself."

"And what ill current in the black tides brings you here?"

"May I enter?"

"Shall I invite demons over my threshold?"

"I am no demon. See you? I wear iron amulets designed to repel demons, and my entering your place will not make it any more hospitable to foul things."

Sonja scowled doubtfully for a moment; then, remembering that the room had already proven vulnerable to one foul being at least, she stepped back and nodded. Areel crossed the threshold, and Sonja shut the door after her.

Lera, trembling visibly at sight of her mistress, stepped back and nearly tripped onto the bed. Chost lifted an arm about her shoulders, steadying her, reminding her that he was there.

Areel glanced at the two youngsters, then pivoted to confront Sonja. The Hyrkanian stood at the door, hand on sword-hilt, half-crouched in a stance that could carry her into a lunge and thrust at the first breath of betrayal; her left hand was at her belt-pouch. Areel marked it all.

"What, then?" Sonja asked her. "You come for the talisman?"

"For the talisman, and more. You own it; I want it. But I want it only to battle a common enemy."

"Nalor? I don't see how—"

"Nalor, yes, but Kus most of all."

"Ah, I see. The *ilorku.*"

"Aye, the vampire. Nalor I can destroy, but my revenge does not stop there. I must also destroy that which my father died trying to slay."

"Revenge has a way of not stopping at all."

"I came to make a proposal, Red Sonja. I want the talisman. Since I know that you will never give it to me of your own choice, I want your help."

Sonja snorted derisively. "I trust you, Areel, about as far as I could throw you straight up."

"Nor do I trust you, Sonja. That understood, let us recognize that we both face an enemy—Kus—who may well destroy us if we do not unite against him."

Sonja's vigilance did not abate as Areel spoke. She stole a glance at Lera and Chost—both apparently balanced on a precarious cliffside of emotions—then back to the sorceress. "So war and politics do, indeed, make for strange partnerships, eh, Areel? I can't deny the truth of what you're saying. Only, I still don't trust you."

"Can you listen to me long enough to hear a plan of mine?"

"If that plan doesn't put my life in your hands, even for a heartbeat."

"It may save both of our lives, Red Sonja. It could succeed if we cooperate; otherwise. . . ."

Sonja nodded. "Very well. I'll listen. Chost, I need some wine. Would you pour?"

"Yes, Sonja."

"Areel, have a seat—that wooden chair. And I warn you, make no sudden moves, utter no uncommon syllables—or I'll pull out this talisman and wither you."

"I sense its power even now, Sonja. Its strength goes to whomever possesses it. I am not powerful enough to attack you in this room, where your strength resides."

Chost crossed the room and handed Sonja a cup of wine. She sipped, then asked Areel: "Will you have some?"

"No."

Sonja drank it down, smacked her lips, set aside the cup. "To your plan, then. Speak."

"If you agree to it, Sonja, I ask only that we follow through immediately—today, this very afternoon."

Sonja nodded. "If that seems best. Now, out with it."

Areel explained her plan quickly and succinctly, and Sonja found herself nodding in agreement all along, save for a point here and there where she suggested emendations. When the sorceress was finished, Sonja stood up, having already decided to follow through at once.

"Chost—Lera—you are not to come with us or follow us," she cautioned the youngsters. "Remain here in the room, and if we do not return by nightfall, go to the authorities and report to them that murder has been committed at Lord Nalor's, and get a troop of city guards to the north end as quickly as possible. . . ."

It was past mid-afternoon. The streets were busy, and the front offices of Lord Nalor's apartment were likewise busy—with messengers, public officials, servants and administrators. Guards at the front portal nodded in silence to those entering and exiting, but called a halt to one tall, red-haired woman in armor who was mounting the steps with two hired servants close behind her. Between them the servants carried a large, rolled carpet.

"State your name," said the commander of the guard.

"I am called Red Sonja, of Hyrkania."

"What's your business with Lord Count Nalor?"

"My business is for his ears alone."

"Young woman, you go no farther unless you answer my—"

"Kus," said Sonja in a low but intense voice.

"What?"

"It has to do with Kus, the magician. I suggest you

allow me to bring this carpet into Lord Nalor's presence immediately."

"This has to do with Lord Kus?"

"Call him a lord if you want. I call him a fiend."

"Why was I not told of this?"

"There was no time. This is very urgent."

The guard deliberated for a long moment, shared eyes with his comrades at the door. "Very well," he decided. "Tell your men to set down the carpet. My men will carry it in and accompany you."

Sonja's servants put the carpet down; she paid them and dispatched them.

The guard commandant knelt to the rolled rug. "I think I'd better inspect this—"

In a heartbeat Sonja's arm was out and across the carpet. "Don't touch it! It has to do with sorcery! Do you think I'd risk my life bringing this damned thing here, unless I were under the orders of Nalor himself?"

Astounded, the guard straightened up. "Sorcery? What in Mitra's name are you saying?"

"This can't wait, damn it!" Sonja spat at him. "The day is dying—nightfall will shortly come. We can't waste any more time! Just take me to Nalor!"

Still the guard did not move.

"Have two men carry this rug to your master. Hurry! In an hour you'll bless my rudeness!"

Sonja's insistent manner decided the guard. Strange rumors had been circulating about Kus and his true nature, and this might have something to do with them. At any rate, if this were a ruse, no one woman with a rolled carpet could stand against the small army of guards in Nalor's house.

"Enrir—" The commandant nodded to the man next to him. Together they lifted the carpet to their shoulders. "It feels heavier than any carpet should."

"There are bones in it," Sonja told him matter-of-factly. "Bones from the age of Acheron, turned to iron by Time."

The guards swallowed; sweat blossomed on their brows.

"Now—please—lead me to Lord Nalor."

"He is taking his afternoon rest. . . ."

"I think not. He'll be expecting me."

Down several hallways and up a short flight of stairs they went, the two guards in the forefront, Sonja following with eyes casting in every direction, senses alert as a stalking panther's. Her mind was working furiously. *Tammuz aid me if this ruse fails half-way through. . . .*

Two other guards were positioned at the door to Nalor's resting chamber. At a nod from the day's commandant, they bowed and pulled on the handles. A long scarlet rug led down the center of the room to a stone dais upon which sat an ornate, pillowed divan—and upon the divan, reclining but awake and alert, was Nalor, who now sat up to witness the intrusion.

"What is going on here?"

"My lord," said the commandant, "this woman—"

"I know you! I know you!" cried the nobleman suddenly.

"I'm Red Sonja, Lord Nalor," she responded, while the guards set down the carpet.

"What is the meaning of this?" Nalor was down the dais steps and confronting Sonja from across the room.

The commandant laid a hand on his sword-pommel. "My lord, were you not expecting this—?"

"Lord Nalor," said Sonja quickly, "this intrusion is necessary. Within this carpet I have the weapon that can battle, and defeat, Kus the *ilorku.*"

"What?" Nalor fell back a step in astonishment.

"Aye. It is true. I've known from the first that Kus was a vampire, as you well know. I've suspected, too, that he must have some control over you. Humans do not control one who is both sorcerer and *ilorku.*"

"Silence, woman!" snapped Nalor, glancing at his guards, who were fidgeting uneasily. "Yet—if you truly possess a weapon to battle him. . . ." The nobleman approached, hands out and trembling, reaching for the carpet.

"Hold a moment!" Sonja warned him. "Precautions must be taken. Witness this." From her belt she withdrew the talisman, which began to glow softly in her hand. "This protects me, Lord Nalor. Stand close by, and it will protect you likewise. But I cannot answer for your guards."

Nalor glanced at them.

"They had best retire outside the door."

Nalor looked suspiciously at Sonja. "How do I know that I can trust you?"

"Do you fear one woman? Your guards'll be within earshot if you need them. But I cannot guarantee their safety if they remain close to the power of what is wrapped in this rug. Magic against Kus. . . ."

Nalor took a deep breath. What had he to lose? The vampire would be coming for him soon; this was his last hope.

"Outside," he told the four guards. "Wait near the door—and do not close it entirely. I will call for you, if it is necessary." Then, when they seemed to hesitate: "Move! Go, now!"

All four went out, closing the door behind them but leaving it ajar.

Nalor faced Sonja. "This had better not be a trick."

"Merely a trick to deceive the evil that has been

feasting for so long on Shadizar, Lord Nalor. Stand back, please." Sonja returned the talisman to her belt-pouch, bent to the carpet and grabbed hold of it.

"Wait!" said Nalor. "You said I was to stand near you—"

Sonja yanked the carpet, pulled it back. Nalor stepped out of the way as it unrolled, over and over—then gasped. For as the last of the lush carpet unfurled, Endithor's daughter appeared and jumped to her feet.

For an instant Nalor stared at her, speechless, then at Sonja, a pallor starting into his face.

"At last, Lord Nalor!" Areel hissed.

Nalor reached for his sword, opened his mouth to yell—but in the same instant Areel lifted her arms straight out, fists clenched, and muttered a word. The nobleman shivered and trembled; a slight whistling, vibrating sound arose. Then Areel, still holding her clenched fists in Nalor's direction, turned her head and snapped:

"Sonja—bar the door!"

Sonja slammed the door shut and brought down the heavy wooden bolt that secured it. From the other side she could hear the soldiers' cries of protest, followed by the poundings of fists. Sonja called to them: "Silence! It is necessary! Your master wishes it."

The pounding ceased, but Sonja knew the guards were not fooled. They would be at the door with heavy tools before long. She cursed, then prayed silently that Areel's plan was not just a delusion born of madness. . . .

Nalor stood rigid, unprotesting, numbed by Areel's sorcery, unable to move. Sweat sprang up on his flesh as he realized his helplessness; his eyes, straining this way and that in their sockets, darted from Sonja to Areel to the weapon-rack.

The sorceress approached the nobleman and stood

before him. "Slayer of my father," she hissed, "here is my father's vengeance!" She clenched her fists more tightly, held them close to Nalor's chest. The whining sound intensified. Nalor, frozen, shuddered in his boots; his eyes went wide; the sweat coated his face and arms. "And soon, dog, your soul shall know the unending torment of the Hells!"

Sonja growled: "Hurry, Areel. Find out what we want to know, then release him. We have little time!"

Still staring Nalor in the eyes: "In my own time, Red Sonja. This moment shall not be hurried; I have waited too long for it."

Sonja stepped forward, keeping her voice low lest the guards be further aroused. "We haven't the *time,* damn it!"

Areel turned her eyes to Sonja; the yellow glow was back in them, like a fire of hate. "And I said, this moment is mine."

"Do you think those guards will wait forever?"

"This man ordered my father torn apart, limb by limb, strip of flesh by strip of—"

"Do you want him, or Kus?"

"I want both!" Areel turned again to the nobleman. "I am going to loosen my sorcerous hold just a little, Nalor—enough to allow you to speak. If you try to rouse your guards, you will die in utter agony. But if you tell me what I wish to know, your death will be quick. Understood? Yes, yes—of course it is. We all want to be without pain—to live without it—as my father wanted to live. . . ."

"Hurry, Areel!" hissed Sonja.

The sorceress slightly relaxed her fists; the slow, low whining sound grew less. Nalor shuddered a bit; his tense muscles became less rigid. He swallowed with a crisp, audible sound—then opened his mouth to scream—

Areel tightened her fists again, this time with her index fingers pointed forward, and uttered a word. Sonja saw a filament of light dart from each extended fingertip and touch Nalor on the chest—and immediately his face contorted with pain. Unable to scream, he sank to his knees, eyes rolling, features twisting as if in terrible agony. Then Areel unclenched her hands—and Nalor fell forward.

"The pain of the Hells!" hissed Areel. "You felt it now, but only briefly and upon only a tiny part of your flesh. Imagine how it will be, Nalor, to feel it within your entire being throughout all eternity! Imagine it, Nalor!"

The nobleman writhed on the floor, gasping, bathed in sweat. Weakly he strove to rise, trembling, his eyes wide in terror.

"Now," Areel whispered, extending her index fingers once more, "where is Kus?"

"In—the cellars," wheezed Nalor. "Sarcophagus. . . ."

"How do we get there?"

"Through—that door—behind. Locked. I have—key."

Sonja, somewhat shaken by what she had witnessed, stooped quickly and rifled Nalor's vest until she came across a key ring; she held it up before Nalor's eyes and turned down the keys, one by one, until he gurgled: "That—one."

"Now," said Areel, "tell us exactly which chamber in the cellars."

"All the way—down. Long passage—next to last—on right."

"Good." Areel stepped back, clenched her fists, and Nalor froze again. The whining sound rose in pitch.

"Hurry, Areel." Sonja crossed the chamber, tested

186

the key in the lock, pushed open the door. "Hurry. Daylight won't linger."

Areel did not follow. Sonja heard Nalor try to grunt. She pivoted sharply on her heels, saw the sorceress standing tall and vengeful, mumbling strange words, lifting both her arms and lowering them, aiming her fists again at Nalor—and suddenly unclenching them, extending all her fingers.

The whining sound—ten gleaming filaments of fire—Nalor's eyes widening—widening. . . .

"Die!" screamed Areel, her eyes blazing with hate. *"Die forever in the Hells!"*

Then even Areel's vengeful scream was drowned out utterly by the awful shriek of pain and terror that burst from Nalor's throat. For an instant Sonja froze in fear. As often as she had heard cries of death and agony in battle, she had never before heard such desperate frenzy in any human voice—as if Nalor felt himself to be riding down cataracts of fire into the eternal boiling thunder of the Hells.

Frozen half-way through the door, she saw him fall backwards, unable to stop himself. He landed on his back with a loud thud, and Sonja somehow knew he was dead even before he struck the tiles. She looked to Areel, trying to hide her fear, knowing she would never be used to sorcery no matter how often she witnessed it.

"Why did you not simply slay him?" she gasped.

"Death," said Areel, "is simply a form of release, is it not? I did not want my father's murderer to get off so easily."

"And did you really send his soul to—to the—?"

"I hope so!" Areel snarled. "But if not, at least *he* thought so!"

There came a heavy pounding on the door from the guards. Areel turned toward the noise, clenching her fists.

"Come on!" Sonja yelled to her. "If they get in, we can't fight them all. Come on, damn you!"

Areel went past her and began to descend the steps. Sonja closed the door and re-locked it from within.

Down the steps they hurried, in dismal darkness. On a lower landing they found a marked candle burning in a bronze sconce, and Sonja saw that the flame had reached the mark that indicated sunset. Nearby was a bracketed torch; Sonja took it and lit it with the candle flame. Then they continued down and down, around and around, to the lowest levels.

"Here," Areel said somberly, leading the way, seeming to need no light. Sonja's torch soon showed the end of the gallery, and several doorways opening blackly from it. They hurried on.

"Wait," cautioned Sonja. "If he's already awake—"

"This one," Areel said suddenly, standing before an open door. She did not enter, however. "Sonja, give me the talisman."

"No."

Areel faced her. The torchlight added a glamour of surrealism to the witch's beautiful oval face, framed with black hair tinged with coppery red from the flames. "Sonja. . . ."

"I'll keep it. It will protect us both. Now, let's go in—but be careful."

Areel crossed her hands, held them to her breast, muttered a protective spell—and entered. Sonja followed with the torch. The stone sarcophagus was there, against the farther wall, with its lid in place.

They hurried forward and began to push against the lid. It slid back without too much trouble, as if it had already been loosened. Sonja raised her torch—and its light revealed an empty coffin.

"Nalor lied!" Areel hissed.

"No—maybe not. He may have truly believed Kus to be here. But the un-dead can be crafty. He may have changed locales."

"Then we must hunt him out."

Sonja shook her head. "There's a worse possibility: twilight may have fallen already. We can't chance it, Areel."

"We must find him!" she insisted angrily.

"He'll find us, more likely," Sonja answered her. "We can't risk hunting for him down here, in his very lair. Kus will find us—he's after us. *Let* him come to us, Areel."

The witch looked at her questioningly.

"We'll return to the apartment," Sonja continued. "Kus may come there to find Nalor; if so, he'll find us waiting instead. But I think we'd better be out of these crypts."

Quietly they retraced their steps up the long stairs to Nalor's chamber. At the entrance door Sonja paused; cautioning Areel to silence, she placed the torch in a sconce on the wall, listening for noises on the other side.

"What do you hear?" Areel asked her. "The guards?"

Sonja crouched, looked through the keyhole. "The guards, all right. They've broken into the room and are gathered around Nalor's body."

"Open the door. I can confound them with sorcery."

But Sonja held her back. "No. Not yet. Not yet. . . ."

"But you said time was of the—"

"Shh, listen to me, Areel!" Sonja was silent for a moment, thinking. She bent again to the keyhole, then straightened. "You didn't see any other doors on the way down those steps, did you? No . . . neither did I.

Now, listen. It's still twilight out there, so even if Kus is already prowling about he's probably still somewhere in the cellars. He may come up this way to meet with Nalor. If he does, we can confront him."

"You mean—you want to wait for him?"

Sonja nodded. "Even with my sword-skill and your witchcraft, I don't want to battle every soldier in Nalor's house while daylight lingers. Just hold on a while; it'll be fully dark before long. Then, if Kus doesn't show, you can cast your illusions and we'll get out of here. But if we make ourselves known now, we may not get a chance at Kus."

Areel made no objections; Sonja sensed that the witch was as exhausted and strained as she was herself —uncertain, angry, with emotions straining at the bit. It would truly be better, in that case, to wait and think things through.

Making as little noise as possible, Sonja eased herself to the floor and sat cross-legged. "Sit down," she advised Areel. "If we're going to wait here, we might as well be resting as comfortably as possible."

Areel sat, not replying.

Sonja sighed, glanced again through the keyhole, then stretched back—and wondered, for a moment, if she had indeed anticipated Kus correctly. . . .

Wondered if, indeed, they would slay the vampire tonight—or wake up tomorrow, themselves pale and lifeless, with new hungers, with new homes in stone sarcophagi buried in cellars in the earth. . . .

An hour before dusk, Chost decided that he could safely leave Lera alone for a few moments while he went on an errand.

"What are you doing?" Lera asked him petulantly. "Don't—don't leave me here. Something might happen. . . . Chost!"

"Don't worry. Nothing will happen. You're safe—as safe as you can be for now." He lay her back on the bed, his hands gentle, reassuring. "Relax, Lera," he urged. "You'll be all right. I won't be gone long."

"But what are you doing?"

"I'm going to get something to help Sonja, if I can."

"But she said—"

"Shhh. Just lie back, Lera. Close your eyes. Rest. I'll be back before you've finished dreaming."

The young lad was so gently insistent, so persuasive, so—so mature, for all his appearance—that Lera, wanting to be able to relax, wanting to escape the worry, sank her head on the pillow and closed her eyes.

Immediately she felt Chost's lips on hers—pressing, full, yet unsure. . . .

She opened her eyes, half-sat up—

And, that quickly, Chost—perhaps self-conscious—was across the room and at the door. "Rest," he reminded her, then vanished down the hall.

Lera, wondering, finding the memory of his kiss pleasant, but not sure just where to place this outcast of the streets in her heart, lay back. She wiggled her toes nervously, stared at the wooden ceiling—sighed. . . .

Closed her eyes. . . .

Opened her eyes, glanced out the window at the waning daylight—and imagined horrors beyond the horrors of her mistress' sorcery. . . .

Imagined Kus, kissing her bloodily—not as Chost had kissed her, safely, carefully, a young boy tasting his first taste of a strange young girl, flush with the first scents of womanhood—

There were footsteps in the hallway—Chost, back before Lera had really noticed the darkness closing down on the world.

She sat up, strangely excited. "What—?"

Chost grinned, closed the door behind him, leaned against it and pulled a dagger from his belt.

"What is that?"

"A knife. An iron knife."

"Where did you get it?"

"From a fool of a merchant. I know my trade."

"Chost—an iron knife?"

He walked towards her, sat beside her on the bed and held the knife in both hands, looking at it somberly. "In case we need it, Lera," he said quietly.

Lera stared at the weapon. It was crude and dark, flecked with rust in a few spots—not a new or quality piece, by any means, yet sturdy and sharp.

"It was partly luck, too," Chost confessed, "—finding an iron weapon so quickly and easily. It was in the back room of a shop just down the street. Probably I'm just being silly, but—just in case we need it. . . ." He hefted the knife, looking now at Lera.

She swallowed, tried to smile; her eyes watered. She dipped her head towards him.

Chost set the knife on the bed, bent to Lera, held her and kissed her—for longer than a moment. . . .

Chapter 10.

In his rest that was not sleep, Kus sometimes had visions—could they be called dreams?—of the past, and sometimes of the future. Just before the dark settled entirely upon Shadizar—just before Kus was animated into an existence that was neither life nor death—he visioned again his death and rebirth. It had happened long ago, in another world.

He remembered the battlefield—the trumpets, the charging horses, the screams, the clashing blades. He remembered the death and agony, the blood, the slaughter—everywhere.

The battlefield—where soldiers slain surely deserved to pass on to their rewards, not to be brought back to earth with their bodies full of strange lusts, their spirits trapped somewhere in a gray world between this world and another.

He had thought himself dead—had remembered dying—but then he had awakened, feeling the succubus at his throat, feeling its long-nailed fingers on his flesh. The sensation was so perfect, so transcendent—like a jewel reflecting all the colors of the rainbow—that Kus, on that battlefield, awakening from death, had shuddered, had orgasmed in his tattered armor as he sat up and embraced the woman-creature—nude, white, cold, black-haired, green-eyed—who kissed him with crimson lips and brought unhuman joy to him. . . .

Then she had ripped herself from his arms and, hissing and snarling, clawing at the ground, had run off—across the moonlit battlefield to feed on the blood of other dead or dying.

Kus, not quite emptied unto death, had arisen, weak but filled with something new that was not life. He had stood up—had surveyed the littered battlefield.

Surely it was the underworld—the battlefield, its piled corpses lit with surreal sheen by the silver and blue light of the broad full moon. The still corpses with the wind whistling over them, with packs of sub-human or half-human things scampering among them—howling things, whispering, sucking and lapping. . . .

He had wandered the night through, feeling the sensations growing within him—the parched feeling. Thinking he needed food, he had tried to eat beef found in a corpse's ration bag—and had vomited it immediately.

Thinking he needed drink, he had tried to undo the stopper on a slain soldier's water skin—and immediately, impelled by some instinct far greater than himself, had cast aside the skin and gripped the corpse's head, twisting it to get at the throat. Then he had bit into the flesh, felt the first rush of salty, tangy blood trickling down his throat, slowly filling him up—filling him until he had become like a bloated leech, a human blood-tick filled with the red life-wine of corpses. . . .

And at the first rays of dawn, he had suffered greater agonies than he had felt when the sword of death had entered his belly on the battlefield.

Sunlight—and not even true sunlight, but only the pre-dawn

light amid the mists that hung over the battlefield—just enough, from the slow turning of the earth, from the inexorable pendulum-swing of the heavens, to scorch his cold flesh to a tingly rash. . . .

Running—frightened by the fear of extermination as he had never feared death in his first life, his true life—Kus had sought safety in a small delve in the rocks with some others of the night.

As the sun rose, he had sunk into himself. . . .

And had awakened at evening to an alarming sense of fatigue and desire—as a leech with dark appetites and intellect, a vampire with a brain and emotions.

He had awakened to the night.

He knew he was dead—animated, though truly dead—when he saw no more in colors. The dead see not in colors; they witness the world in shades of gray.

Even the blood that gave him life was no longer a brilliant crimson stream, but a black flood, as black as the stagnant, moonlit pools in midnight swamps. . . .

He awoke from this memory, this vision, this dream, thirsting anew for the black blood.

He trod through the filthy waters of the city's sewers, came to a grating and reached up, pushed it aside, crawled out. Pulling himself upright, he kicked back the grating and stood silently in the dimness, in the rising moon's light, in the empty street.

He lifted his head, closed his eyes for a moment, saw where he must go—then opened his eyes once more.

Red Sonja's apartment house was down that alley, several blocks away.

Kus walked. His stride was long, but his feet made no sound on the cobblestones.

"Now?" Areel asked Sonja, whispering.

"Aye! Now!" Quickly Sonja worked the key in the

lock, pushed open the door. She stepped into the deserted chamber, Areel following. The door closed behind them of its own accord, locking with a soft click.

Silence. Darkness.

Kus had not appeared. Only shortly before, the guards had removed Lord Nalor's body from the room—to prepare it for burial, possibly, Sonja speculated. She surveyed the chamber. There were two doors besides the one from the passage. One was that from the hallway by which they had originally entered. The second, across the chamber, was a mystery.

And, possibly, a chance for escape.

"Come on, Areel. And be ready, in case we need your witch's strength. . . ."

The door was locked, but it opened to the fourth key on Sonja's chain. It led, not into another hidden recess in the wall, but to a bathing chamber. The fountains were silent and cold now, the torches on the wall unlit.

Creeping close to the wall, Sonja led the way, Areel close behind her. Desperately, she tried to guess the layout of Nalor's apartment building, tried to decide which direction to move. . . .

She stopped.

"What is it?" Areel whispered.

"Listen. . . !"

A door, across from them, opened. Torches lit the large bathing chamber—many torches, carried by many hands. Within moments an army of slaves, escorted by soldiers, were in the echoing chamber.

"Erlik!" Sonja backed against the wall. "They'll see us for certain! Back the way we came!"

They edged along the wall, watching the servants and guards, who seemed to be preparing for a cleaning of the room. Presently they came again to the door. Still watching the guards, Areel worked her hand behind her, unlatched the door and pushed it open.

It creaked.

Areel stepped inside.

Sonja, hissing with exasperation, backed in behind Areel.

"Hey! You! *Stop, there!*"

Sonja jumped in, hearing a metallic clatter as she did so. She kicked closed the door, threw the bolt.

"Too late, witch! They've seen us!"

"Then we must hide in the passage again. Open it, Sonja—quickly!"

Sonja suddenly realized she no longer had the key ring. "Erlik's curse!" she muttered, remembering the metallic clatter. "I've lost the keys. We're trapped!"

It was dark in the rooming house. Twilight had fallen and deepened into night.

Chost waited impatiently, sitting in the chair in a corner of the room. Lera lay upon the bed—asleep, finally. Though Chost glanced at her occasionally, he mainly kept his eye on the window, staring at the darkness, watching as the lamps were lit on the wall outside—wondering when he should go to the city guards and alert them—

Wondering whether he should go to the city guards. . . .

He did not want to—it went against his instincts. Moreover, he felt he had his own score to settle against Kus. Silently he pondered the iron knife in his hands, wondering if he could find courage to use it against the vampire to avenge Stiva.

Stiva. . . .

Chost thought of his friend, remembered how they had discovered one another on the streets at the age of seven—how they had fought each other, stolen together, helped one another out. Stiva—his closest friend. And the way he had died. . . .

Chost, thinking of Stiva, reliving his life with him and the others, seemed to grow drowsy—seemed to fall into a dream of memories. His head fell forward, his eyes still open; though he noticed a darkness at the window obscuring the lamplights from outside, he did not pay attention. He dreamed of Stiva and his lost friendship while, dimly, as though overhearing a conversation from the adjoining room, he watched as the black cloud grew and took shape.

He watched, emotionless, aware yet not aware, as Kus bent over Lera's sleeping form and silently placed a pale hand upon her breast.

Lera's eyes opened, reflecting no fear.

Kus' words issued sibilantly, like a serpent's whisper: "Where is Red Sonja?"

Lera answered him dreamily: "She is gone."

"And where, child, is she gone?"

"To Lord Nalor's."

"And why there?"

"To battle Kus. To slay the vampire."

"She is there now?"

"Yes," murmured Lera. "There, now."

"You are a sweet child. Will you come with me to Lord Nalor's house?"

"I—I am afraid."

"Why are you afraid?"

"I fear sorcerers, and vampires."

"Then, look at me. You do not fear me. Do you think I am a handsome man?"

"Yes. . . . Very handsome."

"Do you love me?"

"Yes. . . . Very much."

"I can protect you. You will have nothing to fear, with me. Come. Into my arms."

Lera sat up, opened her arms, embraced Kus.

He lifted her up, held her in his arms, her soft warm flesh against his stony coldness.

"We will go, now. I will protect you. I will take you to Sonja."

"But what of Chost?"

"Chost is safe. You love me. Come."

"Yes. . . . Yes. . . ."

Chost watched Kus, with Lera in his arms, step onto the window sill, drop into the night. Faintly, he heard the quiet thud of his landing, then his receding footsteps.

Faintly, the memory—like a dream. Faintly, the awakening, the remembering. . . .

He awoke—remembered. Gripping his knife, he ran to the empty bed, then to the window. No Kus.

First, Stiva—and now. . . .

With a hoarse cry of grief and rage, Chost climbed over the sill, dropped the short distance from the window into the alley, and ran northward.

"Erlik!" Sonja yelled. "They've got a battering ram!"

They had bolted the doors with spears from Nalor's weapon collection. Now the resounding crashes at the hallway entrance came again and again—thundering—hammering—making the very walls shake, the floor tremble—

And at the other door, the entrance to the bathing chamber, came the sounds of axes, chopping into the wood around the handle and lock.

Sonja jumped onto the dais, pushed aside the divan, backed herself against the wall and stood, sword out, surveying the room. There she waited, her back to the wall, in the highest accessible point in the room. Looking out the window, she could see guardsmen gathering on the lawn below; there was no escape that way.

Areel joined her, silent as if contemplating, arms uplifted and folded before her breast, amulets dangling and tinkling. She stepped beside Sonja, and as the Hyrkanian kept her eye on the weakening, buckling hallway entrance, so did Areel watch the axe blows bite deeper and deeper through the door of the bathing chamber.

"Sonja. . . ."

"What, Areel?"

"Give me the talisman."

"You aren't touching it!"

"Only my magic can save us now, and I need that—"

"You aren't touching the talisman! Take it from my corpse, witch—but I'll not give it up, otherwise."

Areel looked Sonja in the eyes with burning anger. She trembled with wrath, like a panther about to spring—

But then, with a cascading rush of noise—a splintering of timbers, an upsurge of yells and curses—the door to the hallway burst open. A dozen guards stumbled and lurched into the room, carried along by the impetus of the battering ram they bore—a short column of marble hoisted onto their shoulders. They tumbled in a heap, and around them poured in two dozen more, angry-eyed, snarling, swords and axes bared.

Their leader, a tall man with a twin-pointed beard, lifted a hand and held the others back, then faced Sonja and Areel and cried out:

"You murdered Lord Nalor! Give yourselves up, or we'll slay you here and now!"

But before there was time for a reply the second door burst open, carrying three axes with it, embedded in the wood. In rushed another dozen of Nalor's household troops—and they did not pause.

"At them!" screamed the leader, a red-haired man. "They killed the master!"

Areel shrieked, "Fools!" She half-crouched, lifted her arms, brought them down.

The whining sound filled the air. The red-haired leader was half-way across the chamber, nearly to the dais steps, when the bolt of sorcerous energy struck him full. He shrieked and fell backwards to the floor, a glowing hole in the middle of his breastplate. For a moment he lay kicking, shrieking, his armor clattering, looking like a beetle burned by the concentrated light of a lens. In a moment more his rockings ceased, and from the smoking hole in his chest blood oozed out and stained the flags.

Areel slumped and shuddered; she was white-faced and breathing hard, as though half exhausted from a hard run. But then she rallied and stood tall and proud once more. Crazy-eyed, her features twisted in a snarl, she lifted her arms and wheeled to face the first mob of troops. "Who's next?" she screamed.

Both parties held back, until one voice assured his comrades: "They can't kill all of us at once!"

"I can and will!" Areel shot back. "And whom my sorcery blasts shall know forever the fire of the Hells!"

Still the troops hesitated, mumbling, grumbling, urging each other on, with no one ready to take the first step.

"Come *ahead!*" Areel shrieked, now trembling with such energy that she skipped ahead a few steps, holding up her arms. She laughed maniacally at the poised troops. "I want to send every soul in this room screaming to the Hells! Come! Let me burn your souls in the Hells!"

Sonja glanced at her, wondering if Areel had lost her mind. Evidently she was drawing energy from some supernatural source. *Mitra!* she thought, as a shudder played down her spine. *Has a demon possessed her. . . ?*

"*Fight meeee!*" Areel screamed. "Murderers of my father! Come and taste the Hells!" She barked a wild laugh, lowered her arms at the twin-bearded leader of the first troop—

Suddenly a wind blew through a high window in a corner of the room. Some of the soldiers cried out, pointed. Areel pivoted—and saw a black wind, a cloaked wind with flaming yellow eyes and a death-like face, coalescing into substance.

Kus.

He had jumped or floated in from the window and now stood at the other end of the room, tall and erect, smiling darkly—with Lera, silent, in his arms.

He faced Areel and Sonja. "What's this?" he asked evenly, smiling calmly. His eyes glowed like yellow gems reflecting fire.

"Monster!" Areel howled, moving forward.

With a flourish Kus motioned her back, swinging Lera down with one arm, protectively, so that her feet were on the floor and her blond head on his chest. Her eyes were closed.

"Areel," said the vampire quietly, shaking his head. "Sonja. Give yourselves up—to these troops, or to me; I care not—or I shall slay this child."

Sonja's heart stopped for a moment; her sword lowered involuntarily.

Kus watched Areel. "Give it up, daughter of Endithor."

202

Areel shrieked: "Monster! Corrupter of souls!" She threw up her arms, lowered them extended. *"Die in the Hells!"*

Surprisingly, the force of the swift attack stunned Kus and he was thrown back on his feet. But then, effortlessly, he hurled Lera behind him and stepped ahead. Sonja saw the girl roll on the stone, fetch up roughly against the wall and strike her head on the tiles. She felt a surge of anger, gripped her sword more tightly.

Kus' eyes burned into Areel's. "Foolish thing. . . ." he muttered, and advanced.

The whining sound grew in the air, and a shimmering light appeared between Areel and the sorcerer. The guards, astounded, lowered their weapons, dropped back. Sonja edged back also, lifting her blade—

And Areel, faced now with a power far greater than her own, whimpered—gasped—tightened her fists till her arms trembled.

Kus hissed from his throat, and continued to advance.

The whining sound grew so intense that some of the soldiers covered their ears. Sonja bent her head to the wall, clenching her teeth.

Kus placed a foot upon the first step of the dais.

And now, as the whining shrilled, as the energy filled the room, both Kus and Areel began to glow—whitely, intensely, their bodies shimmering with an unreal kind of heat or force.

Abruptly, arrases and curtains in the room burst into flames—slow flames that ate their way leisurely up the bottom of the hangings, singeing, scorching, smoking.

Urns and braziers in the chamber began to shudder and tinkle, wobbling on metal legs. The very flags of the floor began to tremble, to rock, and in the joints between them smoke appeared; the old cement hissed and smoked, sent up gray clouds, began to crumble. . . .

Areel suddenly shrieked like a dying, tormented soul ripped by demons.

Kus laughed and strode ahead, yellow eyes leering in triumph. Areel's shriek continued, rose higher and filled the room as she threw up her arms—as she fell into a crouch—as she swooned and leaned to one side—

Kus reached out; his palms, flat and open, touched the sides of her head. His long fingers curled and clenched—and Areel's skull suddenly crumpled inward in a slow, crimson burst of blood, brains, bone, flesh.

Kus threw back his head and laughed.

Areel's corpse, the pulped head half-twisted from it, rolled limply down the dais steps to the floor, gushering blood.

Kus flicked his hands sharply; crimson wetness sprayed from his claws in a shower of droplets.

"Now!" he yelled, turning to Sonja. *"Now!"*

She moved. Swiftly, without thought, acting purely on instinct, on fear, she pulled the talisman from her belt, wrapped its chain about her sword-hilt and pointed the weapon directly at the vampire's throat—

Kus shrieked. The glow of the talisman swept across his features, driving him back. Down the dais steps he retreated, to the floor, where he turned to the horrified guards in the room, lifted his arms and howled: "Slay her! I command you! Feel my power, and obey my will! Slay her!"

"Sonja!"

Chost's voice! She looked up. At the window near the dais was Chost—jumping now from the high sill. Kus, beneath the window, looked around, half turned—

The boy landed on the floor, pushed himself forward in a rebound. Kus' talons swept out, clutching for him—but Chost, remaining low, nimbly bounded past the sorcerer. His slender arm drove out as he ran by, and the dark iron knife in his hand ripped Kus' robe—and flesh.

The sorcerer shrieked in agony and leapt forward. Blood dripped from his legs to the tiles, and he nearly fell to his knees.

Chost ran to Lera and crouched by her. "Wake up, Lera!" he yelled, grabbing her by the armpits and dragging her across the floor. Kus strode toward him, talons reaching, yellow eyes burning with infernal rage.

"Kus!" Sonja screamed furiously, and hurled herself across the dais and down the steps, sword extended.

The sorcerer saw her coming, threw himself back from the dais—away from the talisman-charged blade.

Sonja checked her headlong rush, then took the last of the stairs deliberately, one at a time, slowly, cautiously. Kus cringed back and away from her, crawled into the stone corner beneath the window and curled up there—hissing, bleeding, eyes burning like red mists of Hell glimpsed through cracks in the earth.

"Slay him!" yelled the soldiers in the room. "Slay him!"

But Sonja stood her ground, above Kus, facing him cautiously, tensely, aiming the blade at his throat.

Kus sneered: "That will not slay me."

"I know." Sonja's voice was a guttural ripple of menace.

"Your sword cannot slay me, nor can that talisman."

"I know that," Sonja said. "But it weakens you, Kus. Aye, it weakens you, and it saps your strength, and it limits many of your powers, doesn't it?"

The vampire's eyes blazed fearsomely, flaring a baleful yellow for an instant, but then dying down to a sullen red once more. Sonja shuddered at her close proximity to the creature.

Without taking her eyes from him, she called to the troops in the room: "Get weapons—iron weapons, in Mitra's name! Get swords—spears—knives—anything of iron! Get them wherever you can! Iron weapons wound him!"

Kus hissed and writhed in the corner. Sonja poked her sword at him; he screamed and backed further against the wall.

"And get salt!" she yelled. "Sacks of salt!"

A moment of hesitation; then the twin-bearded soldier ordered: "All of you men wait here. Now, you—you and you—and you—follow me."

They reappeared after several minutes, having ransacked Nalor's kitchen and weapon-racks.

"Surround me," Sonja told them. "Any of you with iron weapons, stand beside me. Don't get too close, and don't look him too long in the eyes. Use spears and swords. Strap those knives to poles, damn it! If you get close to him he'll have you!"

They lined up, seven or eight soldiers beside her, encircling Kus, holding him against the wall.

Chost carried Lera to the divan on the dais. Still she did not awaken. He lay her back, propped her head with pillows, got a bowl of water from a table and rinsed a cloth in it, daubed Lera's hot brow and face with it, dividing his attention between the girl and Sonja and the soldiers.

"Salt," Sonja commanded.

Kus hissed and writhed. Again Sonja felt a surge of horror and disgust at being so close to this dangerous, supernatural reptile, and knew her feelings were shared by all present.

Someone handed her a sack of salt.

"Open it," she told him. Then she reached in, withdrew a handful and held it up. "What does salt do to demons, eh, Kus?'' she asked, her voice quivering with hate.

Kus crouched, lifted his head, reached out his arms and tensed as if to spring. . . .

Sonja flung the salt in his face. The vampire shrieked awfully, deafeningly, grabbed his face in his hands, dug at his flesh as gas and smoke poured up. The salt was burning his flesh, corroding it, eating it away, causing it to bubble like hot tar.

Sonja took a deep breath. "I was never much for torture," she said evenly, "but by Erlik, demon, I'll do that every time you even think to escape!"

"Slay him now," urged one of the soldiers.

"None of this will slay him," Sonja warned. "Iron can wound him, salt will burn him, this talisman weakens him—but only one thing can slay him entirely." She looked up at the open window above the cringing vampire. "We must wait until dawn."

Kus hissed and snarled, and Sonja looked at him with such loathing and hatred as she had seldom experienced in her entire life.

The night-long vigil was a strange experience in nerve-straining anxiety. Never once did Sonja relax her guard; never once did her sword-point veer far from Kus' face or throat, though many times one or another of the house guards offered to take her place that she might rest.

"No." Sonja would shake her head. "I'm all right. I want to see every moment of this through. I want him to look at me and know I am the cause of his doom. Eh, Kus? How long have you lived, you foul coffin-worm? Hey? How many have you killed, or made un-dead like yourself, you leech from Hell?"

Kus would growl and hiss. Once he replied: "Why do

you imagine I am any more master of my fate than you are of yours, Hyrkanian? You think to condemn me, but I and all my kind were once as you. You call me evil, but the same spark of evil is in all humans as well. Your kind is the origin of my kind; the evil is in all of you, and could one day make you even as I am. Condemn me, then, but know that you condemn yourselves as well!"

Yet more often he would try to lull the tiring soldiers with promises of sweet victories, glorious powers, great wealth, mastery over women and immortality. At every instance, Sonja or someone else would prod him with blades or cast a pinch of salt upon him, and the vampire would screech and writhe, and try to back farther into the corner.

Oil lamps burned low in the room as the night went on. New ones were lit, or the oil replenished.

Some in the room, among those not standing guard over the vampire, would begin to doze—then start awake in a sweat of fear. Others tried to play at cards or dice, but found they could not concentrate. The air of fear in the room was too great. The guardsmen remembered too vividly that moment when Kus had nearly taken control of their minds to cause them to attack Sonja—the horror of feeling their wills slipping away, of the monstrous presence of the un-dead even now in this very chamber. And some remarked on what might have happened had not a small lad with an iron dagger come leaping through the window.

Chost was fortifying himself with wine and bread brought from the kitchen; he stayed close to Lera, often feeling her pulse, and prayed that by morning her numb condition would change. Her nostrils flared but slightly, her breast rose and fell with the same slow, steady rhythm, unchanging. What had Kus done to her? Would she ever awake. . . ?

Kus watched Chost and tried to play upon his fears. "You realize, don't you, boy, that if they slay me, her soul shall go with me also."

"Shut up, hell-spawn!"

"It is true!" Kus laughed hollowly. "It is true!"

"Be quiet!" Chost sprang up, lifted his iron knife.

"Chost!" Sonja yelled to him, then poked at Kus with her sword. The sorcerer hissed and growled obscenities at her, tried to grab the blade in his hands; but the metal was white-hot to him, and he ripped his hands away with a howl of agony.

The night wore on. Other soldiers in the room traded places with those beside Sonja. One, of a philosophical bent, questioned Kus quite seriously.

"How long have you lived, *ilorku*?"

Kus only growled.

"Come; tell me. I am intrigued. How long have you been alive?"

"Your great grandmother sucked my blood during the rites of Semrog, fool. I ravished her, and she willingly bent to dogs when I ordered her to."

Unrattled, the soldier laughed at him. "Seriously, tell me. Do you remember King Atron?"

"Is he some hero of yours? He was filth! Filth!"

"Do you remember ancient Acheron? I want to know."

Kus' mood changed. "I dwelt amid the purple shadows of Python, Acheron's capital," he said quietly. "I am as old as some of the gods you fools worship. You are slaying a deity, don't you know that? This is all a futile effort on your part. I will return even from the dust. I did so, once. . . ."

Sonja lifted a brow. Kus seemed weak, drawn; he had gone all night without blood-sustenance. Was his mind straying?

"I am the god of dark forests," he breathed, closing his eyes and letting his head sink back. "Do you know how many lives have passed through me? I have devoured nations—whole tribes and nations. Yet they come on. Like the rain, like the green things, like all things—they come on, with new life, new blood. . . . *Why?*" he suddenly screamed, opening his red eyes, full of hatred. "*Why?* Why should you trivial, ephemeral creatures live and die in ignorance while the gods damn me? Don't you realize the knowledge, the wisdom—?"

He tried to sit up, tried to grab again at Sonja's blade. A soldier stabbed him with iron. Kus shrieked; he fell back, kicking his heels on the stone, slapping his burnt hands on the brick. Then he laughed, from low in his throat.

He opened his eyes wider; their glow had dimmed. "You need me," he hissed, looking at Sonja, at all of them. "Don't you know what I am? I am the evil you disown within yourselves. What will you do without me? Without me to hate, you must come to recognize your own hatefulness. Your lives will be pointless. What good will be your gods to you, if you destroy me? They will damn you with your own judgement. Humans! Worms! Yours are not true lives; you are shadows. You are as gray and meaningless and fleet as the mists. I alone could give you *true* life!" And then, in a hoarse wail: "Slay me now! In the names of Ordru and Semrog, damn you, slay me now! Now! Don't let me see the sunlight! *Don't let me die in the sunlight!*"

Sonja looked up. Her legs felt wooden from the long ordeal; her back was numb, her arms heavy as lead; her eyes and brain enfeebled, strained.

It was gray, outside the window.

She heard the temple bells in the city, pealing to announce the coming of daylight. Far away, somewhere in Nalor's gardens, cocks crowed.

Kus shuddered. He tried to stand, but was forced back. His face—blistered, pale, raw and black in spots—shivered like drying clay. "Hide me!" he screamed. "Don't let me die in the sunlight, in Ordru's name!"

The soldiers gripped their spears and swords more tightly. Those not already guarding Kus stood up and silently approached the guarded corner. Two dozen stepped up onto the dais, lined the stairs and looked down.

The gray of dawn became brighter. Nervous shufflings filled the room. Chost felt Lera's pulse, held onto her wrist.

"Don't let me die!" Kus screamed. "I am not mortal—you know not what a life you are destroying. You know nothing of me, yet you *are* me! Don't let me die-iiieeee!"

White filled the window. Sonja whispered solemnly: "Stand back, now, all of you. . . ."

Kus stood up slowly, crouched as if for a desperate spring. His eyes, dimmed from their brilliant yellow, showed white, with small gray pupils. His lean hands clutched at the brick walls, his taloned feet bent on the tiles.

A wide bar of golden sunlight brightened at the window, blossomed in a distorted rectangle on the far wall near the floor.

Kus took in a wild, choked breath. "Don't let me—!"

Then, slowly, he sank down, shuddering, writhing and hissing—like a dying serpent, it almost seemed. A mist issued from him.

Sonja took a deep breath. "Stand back. Stand back, I said."

The others around her stepped away, and Sonja advanced. Lifting her sword, she pointed it at Kus' breast, shoved it in partially. She felt little resistance there; it was as though she had stabbed a sack of straw.

With a thrust she forced Kus away from the corner. He was hissing and rasping as if too weak to shriek or yell, retreating from the sword as from a hot iron. Suddenly he collapsed, face down, in the rectangle of sunlight at the base of the other wall.

Sonja stood back and watched.

Mist began to grow up from the body of the vampire. He struggled weakly beneath his dark robe for a moment, moving one arm forward, twitching one leg. Then he moved no more, and the sunlight on his burnt flesh glowed whitely; his hair fell away, white and powdery; the flesh of his hands peeled away like dried parchment, and the bones collapsed into small white puddles of fine dust. The skull, last of all, crumbled away into a brown pile of clumps, then dissolved into more pools of powder. The dark robe and other clothing settled down to the floor, atop nothing but dust.

Silence, profound, in the chamber.

Sonja breathed deeply, shudderingly, then took up an oil lamp. Returning with it to where Kus' ashes and clothes lay sprawled on the stone, she dropped it into the pile. Oil splashed, flames jumped up—and quickly a black, stinking fire was burning away all traces of the old dust.

On the dais, Chost's heart leapt. Beneath his hands he felt Lera's pulse quickening. Her eyes fluttered. He put his hands to her hair, felt her face flushing, listened to her take in a breath. Then she opened her eyes, looked into his.

"Chost. . . ."

Sonja walked slowly to a chair and sat down, utterly exhausted. She reached for a wine pitcher, and the bronze vessel clattered against the silver cup, betraying her nervousness. Quickly she gulped down her wine, threw back her head and emitted a long, weary sigh.

EPILOGUE:
Love—and a Talisman

The Municipal Board of Inquiry of the city of Shadizar—an arm of the city council instituted immediately when word of both Nalor and Kus' deaths were announced—spent three days examining evidence and testimony concerning what had happened and who had been involved. Its findings were ordered hidden away in some obscure corner of the city archives, and on pain of fine or banishment·or both it was made clear that no one involved was to speak at all of the matter.

Fine or banishment notwithstanding, rumor and gossip soon spread the tale into every alley and tavern in Shadizar.

Sonja's testimony had swayed the hearing. Her own innocence in the matter was accepted unquestionably when the urgent reasons for her ruse against Nalor and his servants were made abundantly clear. Her own words, and those of the servants and guards of Nalor's household, proclaimed her innocent of any plot to slay Nalor. Areel, Endithor's daughter, had slain the Councillor—obviously by magic, for no wound was found on him.

One result of the inquiry was that a further inquiry was ordered to be made into the late Lord Nalor's illegal doings while holding his governmental post. And, with that, Sonja was free to go. "These incidents," piously proclaimed one of the white-bearded justices on the board, "show clearly how evil is like unto the moral image of it presented by our scholars and theologians: 'The serpent blindly followeth its evil instincts, devouring itself from tail to head, destroying itself in its own perverse frenzy.' "

Free to go—and free, too, to collect the reward money.

Shadizar had put up one hundred gold pieces for the arrest of the criminal responsible for the throat-tearing murders. But Sonja refused to keep the money entirely for herself. When at last her testimony was recorded and she found herself free to go, she met Chost and Lera in a square and gave them fully half her reward.

They hardly refused her largesse, though they seemed slightly embarrassed by it.

"You two deserve it," she told them frankly. "Whether you intended it or not, your actions made it happen."

They walked through the square, talked, shared a bottle of wine.

"Staying in the city?" Sonja asked them.

Chost shook his head. "We're headed west," he assured her.

Lera smiled and squeezed his hand.

"We've had enough of this city for a while," Chost went on. "And this gold may make an honest man of me." Sonja cocked an eye to him. "Well—for a time," Chost demurred.

Lera laughed.

Sonja asked: "And what of you, Lera? No scars?"

215

"Plenty of them, Sonja. But—" She leaned on Chost, rubbed her hair on his shoulder. "Good things, too."

"She won't be acting the maid-servant again," Chost asserted. "I promise you that! When I return to roguery, I'll do it in some form of commercial business. Then someday, when I return to Shadizar, it won't be as a beggar and a thief, and I can help out all who were friends to me here."

Sonja smiled. "I hope it works out that way. Aye. Aye, but put all this behind you for now." And then: "Come, Chost. It's nearly lunchtime, and before I head out, I'll let you buy me a meal. It's the least you can do to pay me back for all that bread and cheese you devoured."

She rode out that evening with a purse full of gold, the dust of Shadizar washed from her, her armor cleaned, her weapons shining. Nor did she wait for that caravan she had signed aboard. That would have meant escaping from Shadizar in the company of Shadizar, and one of the rewards of her aloneness, Sonja felt, was the freedom to ride on when the action was done, to leave behind what had happened, to put distance between memories and herself.

She headed southwest, on a well-travelled road leading into the continent—a road she had travelled before. She did not go far, this night, for a light rain came up, and she was tired from her vigil of the night in Nalor's mansion, plus the testimony that had followed. Stopping at an inn, she first saw to her horse, then entered and ordered a meal.

And as she ate, sights in the tavern reminded her of the past week, and Sonja wondered indeed how she might leave that time in Shadizar behind.

Men in the corner were throwing knives at the bull's eye—one of them with the same young laugh that used to possess Sendes. There was also a tall, lean man in a dark robe—a scholar and no sorcerer, but with something of the light of the otherworld beneath his brows.

And there was a stout red-haired woman sitting at a middle table, with a young man at her side, his hair sandy-colored. Not herself, and not Chost—yet there was enough in that image, in Sonja's current frame of mind, to bring back the sleeping young Chost in her room in a rundown old house in Shadizar.

She bought a second bottle of wine and headed upstairs to her room, then sat on her bed and drank it slowly while the strains of a singer and his lute-strumming echoed up from below.

Sonja had not cried herself to sleep since reaching womanhood; but tonight, as the wine and the exhaustion put her under the covers, she dreamed back to Hyrkania—to her father and mother and brothers—to the farm, the red-haired people, the good times, the laughter and the songs, the hopes and ambitions—

—and in her dreams, she saw herself again as a young girl, Lera's age, crying for happiness at the sight of her father and mother by the fireplace in their farmhouse.

Crying—but happy, content. A young woman again, dreaming unshadowed dreams.

And how many roads, she wondered, would she follow before she reached that place again, with her sword that weighed more heavily on her soul than any curse the gods might place on the soul of a dying vampire?

Stories

☞ of ☜

Swords and Sorcery

Available wherever paperbacks are sold or use this coupon.

ALL TWELVE TITLES AVAILABLE FROM ACE
$2.25 EACH

- [ ] 11630 **CONAN, #1**
- [ ] 11631 **CONAN OF CIMMERIA, #2**
- [ ] 11632 **CONAN THE FREEBOOTER, #3**
- [ ] 11633 **CONAN THE WANDERER, #4**
- [ ] 11634 **CONAN THE ADVENTURER, #5**
- [ ] 11635 **CONAN THE BUCCANEER, #6**
- [ ] 11636 **CONAN THE WARRIOR, #7**
- [ ] 11637 **CONAN THE USURPER, #8**
- [ ] 11638 **CONAN THE CONQUEROR, #9**
- [ ] 11639 **CONAN THE AVENGER, #10**
- [ ] 11640 **CONAN OF AQUILONIA, #11**
- [ ] 11641 **CONAN OF THE ISLES, #12**

Available wherever paperbacks are sold or use this coupon.